DAISY

Also by Marion Chesney:

MY DEAR DUCHESS
LADY MARGERY'S INTRIGUES
HENRIETTA
KITTY

Marion Chesney

Daisy

Macdonald Futura Publishers

A Futura Book

First published in Great Britain in 1981
by Macdonald Futura Publishers Ltd

ISBN 0 7088 2017 4
Printed and bound in Great Britain by
©ollins, Glasgow

Macdonald Futura Publishers Ltd
Paulton House, 8 Shepherdess Walk
London N1 7LW

For Harry Scott Gibbons
and Charles David Bravos Gibbons
with all my love.

DAISY

Chapter One

The very leaves out here seem to be different, thought Daisy Jenkins, clutching hold of her friend's arm. They spread out on the ground before them, sparkling red and gold in the autumn sunshine. Not like the rusty plebeian kind that carpeted the town of Upper Featherington, now uncomfortably a long way behind.

"We shouldn't ought to be doing this," said Daisy for the hundredth time. Her friend Amy tossed her blonde curls. "Nobody's going to find out. We're just going to take a peek."

Daisy looked enviously at her friend. Amy Pomfret had a careless, sunny nature and, having made up her mind to play truant from school to spy on the Earl of Nottenstone's house party, she had plunged into the adventure with gay abandon, seemingly free from the dark fears of retribution that haunted Daisy's sensitive mind.

A shy and retiring girl, Daisy had never quite got over being chosen by Miss Amy Pomfret—the most popular girl in the school—to be her best friend. So when Amy had suggested the adventure, Daisy had not had the courage to refuse.

"I think about here will do," said Amy, stopping in front of a curve of moss-covered wall. "Nobody's about. Come along, Daisy, over you go!"

Daisy timidly hitched up her faded tartan skirts to reveal an expanse of cotton petticoat, bleached yellow with age, and a pair of cracked and worn button boots. She nimbly scaled the wall and dropped down on the other side with her heart beating fast. With an energetic thump, her friend joined her.

"Now don't be such a scaredy-cat," whispered Amy. "All we're going to do is creep through the woods to the edge of the garden and have a look at them."

"What if they're not outside?" whispered Daisy.

"Bound to be," said Amy. "Clarrie Johnson's mum has been hired special for the day and she told Clarrie that they takes their tea on the lawn 'round about now."

Daisy's heart jumped into her throat with every popping twig and every crackling movement of their starched petticoats. She almost wished they would be discovered so that the punishment would be swift and fast, for Daisy had been firmly taught by the methodist chapel that the sinner never escaped judgment. And what could be a worse sin than to be found trespassing on the hallowed aristocratic ground of Marsden Castle?

The battlements of the castle suddenly seemed to lean over the trees above them and they could hear the faint sound of voices and laughter. They edged closer and found themselves on the edge of the woods with a vast expanse of lawn rolling out in front of them.

"There they are!" hissed Amy, crouching down behind a bush and pulling Daisy with her.

Daisy drew in her breath in a sharp gasp.

The house party was spread out over the lawn, engaged in a game of croquet. Everyone was dressed in white. The ladies in cascades of white lace, with tiny waists and voluminous hats, and the gentlemen in white flannels and blazers.

Amy put her lips close to Daisy's ear. "That's the Earl and Countess . . . over there."

The handsomest couple Daisy had ever seen stood at the edge of the lawn. The Earl was a tall young man with fair hair the color of ripe corn. His classical features were almost effeminate in their perfection and his eyes, a startling, piercing blue. In complete contrast was the Countess, her masses of heavy black hair almost hidden by an elaborate picture hat of swirling white tulle and artificial flowers. She moved her small body with easy, catlike grace in all the stiff formality of white lace that cascaded in structured layers from throat to hem. She had entangled her croquet mallet in her heavy rope of pearls and was playfully insisting that all the young men of the party should help her.

The rest of the world fled from Daisy's mind as she stared at the enchanted picture . . . at the world of gods and goddesses to which she could never belong. Just for this little while, she, Daisy Jenkins, would imagine that she was part of it. She would dream that she was one of the guests and that in a minute, one of those splendid young men would come searching for her.

The Countess was calling everyone to tea in her high, clear voice when one of the young men gave the croquet ball an energetic swipe with his mallet. It flew toward them, right into the bushes and struck Amy on the leg. Amy sprang to her feet with an undignified shriek and started to hop about.

Daisy got slowly to her feet and then stood frozen with terror. "Flushed two of 'em," yelled the young man. "Hey, Bo, Cecil, Jerry, everybody . . . nymphs in the woods!"

With insolent, languid steps the members of the house party formed a half circle in front of the two girls.

The Countess's enormous brown eyes flicked over the two girls in their shabby tartan dresses. "Schoolgirls," she remarked as if identifying a common type of garden pest. And then without even turning her head, "Curzon . . . take them away."

Daisy's heart sank to her worn boots and she hung her head. Curzon was a leading light of the methodist chapel. Her aunt would hear of it. There was no escape now.

"Oh, do they have to go?" cried a young man with a weak chin, horrendous acne, and an insane giggle. "The blonde one's quite pretty, you know."

Amy gave him a dazzling smile. "Daisy and me just wanted to get a look at you. We didn't mean no harm."

The Earl turned lazily to his wife. "There you are. They didn't mean no harm, my dear."

"They just wanted to see the aristocrats at play," roared a horsey girl. "We've even got a real live Duke for you to gawk at, ain't we? Your Grace, The Most Noble Duke of Oxenden, please present yourself for inspection."

A tall dark man moved to the front of the crowd. Daisy raised her eyes timidly and then lowered them hurriedly. The newcomer had cold, harsh features and eyes of a peculiar, almost yellow, shade. They seemed to bore right into her. "What is your name? You . . . with the brown hair."

"Daisy Jenkins . . . an' please Your Grace." The voice whispered faintly, like the leaves drifting over the immaculate lawns.

The Countess's voice cut across. "Escort these persons off the estate immediately, Curzon. And send Bill from the lodge to report them to their headmistress."

There was a short, shocked silence, punctuated by a few sympathetic murmurs of "I say!" and "Bit hard cheese that," as the two girls were led off by the stern Curzon.

Even the ebullient Amy seemed unnaturally

subdued. At last she burst out. "Oh, Mr. Curzon, do you really have to tell old Meekers about this?" Old Meekers was Miss Margaret Meaken, their headmistress.

Curzon looked down at the two girls from his lofty height, gave a slight cough, and then became surprisingly human.

"I think you have been punished enough, miss, but I've got to do what her ladyship says. She'll check up. She's that sort."

"But she is so beautiful," said Daisy in a subdued voice. She could not believe that such a fairy-tale creature as the Countess would be deliberately malicious.

"Well, it's not for me to discuss my betters," said Curzon repressively. "Let's just leave it that I've got my orders to send Bill from the lodge and that's that." He turned to Daisy. "You're the one that's going to come off the worst. Your aunt isn't going to like this a bit. She worships my lord and lady almost as much as her Maker."

Daisy shuddered. Her aunt, Miss Sarah Jenkins, was a deeply religious spinster who felt that she had been put on earth to go about finding fault with everyone in general and Daisy in particular.

The two girls said good-bye to Curzon and walked off down the road with lagging footsteps and drooping heads. "I'm sorry," said Amy. "It's not so bad for me. My mum will scream and clip me over the ear and then she'll invite all the neighbors in so's I can tell them all about the frocks the nobs were wearing. Will you tell your auntie when you get home?"

Daisy shook her head. "I haven't got the courage. She'll find out soon enough."

She fell silent and the two girls moved slowly through the golden afternoon, each with her own thoughts. A little breeze had sprung up sending cascades of brilliant colored leaves falling across the winding country road. Woodsmoke twisted up lazily from bonfires in the gardens and rooks circled and swirled over the brown, ploughed fields. But Daisy had a nagging feeling that she had been shut out from a fairyland world and that life would never be the same again.

The only way to enter that magic world again would be as a servant. Her aunt, she knew, had been a housemaid. But Sarah Jenkins moralized so much on the sins of the aristocracy and was so reticent about the family for whom she had worked, that Daisy could only assume she had not enjoyed one bit of it.

Her aunt was also peculiarly reticent on the subject of Daisy's parents. Daisy herself could not remember them, and all questions were parried by her aunt's infuriating sniff, followed by a long homily about how she ought to thank God for having a respectable body to take care of her.

When they reached the outskirts of the town, the lamplighter was already making his rounds, leaving pools of gaslight behind him to disperse the evening shadows as he moved slowly down the main street.

The girls came to a halt in front of a forbidding Victorian villa which rejoiced in the name of The Pines. There were no pine trees, only a weather-beaten monkey puzzel and some sooty laurels, but Sarah Jenkins had been in service in Scotland and considered the name to have an appropriate Highland flavor, redolent of grouse shoots and large sprawling picnics on the moors.

Amy opened her mouth to say something and then closed it again. After all, what was there to say? Daisy needs a bit more spirit. Ought to tell that old harridan where to get off. Amy pressed her friend's shoulder sympathetically, and marched off to cope with her own battles.

The stained glass door of The Pines was jerked open as Daisy reached the top step where Sarah Jenkins stood waiting, crackling with starch and bad temper.

She was a very thin, tall, bony woman with black hair scraped painfully back from a fiery red face. Her complexion made her look as if she were in a perpetual temper which, in fact, she nearly always was. She had a large mole at the side of her thin, traplike mouth, with two stiff hairs growing out of it that waved like the antennae of some peculiar bug. As a child, Daisy used to have nightmares that the mole had crept off her aunt's face and had taken on a life of its own and was crawling around the house waving its feelers.

"Dawdling home from school again, you sinner," snapped Miss Jenkins. "Life is one long sinful, idle pleasure for you, miss. Isn't it? You have been looking at boys, haven't you? Lust is in your blood and in your mind, Daisy Jenkins. Isn't it?"

With each sentence she poked the girl in the ribs with a pair of steel knitting needles from which hung a long brown, lumpy scarf. Miss Jenkins knitted brown scarves that she posted off to South Africa for the army, as her contribution to the Boer War. Amy had once been invited to tea and had whispered to Daisy that the army used them to bore the Boers to death. She had gone into convulsions at her own wit and had never been invited again.

"Your tea has been ready this past half hour," remarked Miss Jenkins, giving the unfortunate Daisy a final stab. "And after that, remember to finish your housekeeping duties."

Tea was a silent meal. Daisy usually tried to make some sort of conversation, but she felt crushed down by an overpowering weight of guilt. She hurriedly ate her two slices of doughy white bread and thick burnt crust, two transparent wafers of ham, a miniscule portion of mashed potato, and a nauseating concoction called Russian salad—tinned vegetables mixed with watery mayonnaise.

She carried the dishes downstairs to the kitchen as soon as she was finished, glad to escape from her aunt's basilisklike stare.

The kitchen was dark and cold and smelled of genteel poverty—a mixture of Jeyes fluid and cabbage water.

As she polished the heavy pottery dishes and diligently scrubbed the knives and forks with bath brick, Daisy found the Earl's handsome face constantly in her thoughts. He was the most handsome man she had ever seen. And he had such laughing blue eyes!

Daisy was nearly finishing her studies at St. Cecilia's Parochial School for Girls and had begun, timidly, to notice that mysterious opposite sex. But none of the boys of the town had sparked her imagination like the handsome Earl.

The rest of the evening passed like a thunderstorm, with lightning images of the Earl's laughing face interspersed with heavy clouds of fear and guilt.

Sarah Jenkins did not employ servants, so it was ten o'clock before Daisy thankfully completed her last task—polishing the leaves of the aspidistra that crouched in its brass bowl by the parlor window.

Daisy then went up to her room to hurriedly stuff a blanket along the bottom of the door, so that her aunt would not see the light and know that she was reading in bed. Daisy picked up a copy of Jerome K. Jerome's *Three Men in a Boat* and happily sailed off down the Thames with George and Harris and the dog, Montmorency, and let the worries of reality fade away.

But as she leaned over to blow out her candle—gaslight in the bedrooms was considered a needless extravagance—the face of the Earl appeared before her once more.

Life would never be the same again. Daisy had a feeling that she had turned into a woman all in one day. And she didn't like it one bit.

Chapter Two

The Gods above knew that Daisy Jenkins was about to receive her just punishment. Huge black clouds tumbled across the heavens and icy blasts of wind sent the dead leaves dancing in the corners of the school yard.

Daisy bent over the desks, refilling the ink wells, the weight of fear inside her so heavy that she felt she might topple over. She had dressed with unusual care as though to meet her executioner, her heavy brown hair in two severe braids and her white pinafore gleaming and crackling with starch.

If only she were in one of the noisy lower school classes, bursting at the seams with girls, instead of this rarified upper strata of only seven prim misses. Few parents in Upper Featherington had the money or the inclination to educate a mere girl beyond the year of fourteen. Daisy had some idea that the penny-pinching Miss Sarah Jenkins had kept her on at school so that she might subsequently earn her living as a schoolteacher or governess. A quiet, biddable scholastic girl, she was a great favorite with her teachers and usually enjoyed the dull school routine.

The door of the classroom suddenly burst open with a crash and, without turning her head, Daisy knew that the ax was about to fall.

Miss Meaken's voice rang across the classroom. "Miss Pomfret and Miss Jenkins. To my study immediately."

The moment had arrived and Daisy was glad. Whatever punishment that befell could not be worse than the anticipation of it.

But Amy went white under her freckles and clutched Daisy's arm for support as they hurried down the long corridor. The school had been built on mock ecclesiastical lines and the headmistress's study looked as cosy as a monk's cell. Miss Meaken was seated behind a large refectory desk, with her back to the window where the black clouds tumbled with undisciplined abandon over the deserted hockey pitch.

On hard upright chairs to one side of her sat Miss Jenkins and Amy's mother, Mrs. Pomfret. Miss Jenkins's light-blue eyes searched out Daisy's. They contained a peculiar gleam. Could it be satisfaction? The sinner had finally sinned.

Miss Meaken was a small, dumpy woman encased in herringbone tweed. She wore a stiff, uncompromising wig, and her weak pink eyes peered nervously out at the world from beneath its shadow.

Had she screamed or roared it would have been bad enough. But her voice trembled with unshed tears as she peered through a lorgnette at a crested letter in her hand.

"I was told yesterday, by a message from the lodge boy, of your trespass. This, however, was followed by a letter from the Countess of Nottenstone expressing her strong displeasure. It leaves me with no alternative but to expel you both."

Mrs. Pomfret began to sob noisily and the hairs on Miss Jenkins's mole pointed their accusing fingers at Daisy as she stood with her head bowed, unable to speak or move.

The word "expel" hung in the chilly room like an obscenity.

Amy began to roar and cry like her mother and despite her misery, Daisy could only admire her friend's noisy release.

"You have been a very good pupil, Miss Jenkins . . . one of our best I may say . . ." Miss Meaken was beginning when a housemaid catapulted into the room, her cap askew and her face polished with excitement.

"It's the Dook, mum," she gasped. " 'Is Grace 'imself wants for to talk to you about them." She jerked her cap at the two girls.

Miss Meaken looked at her in a bewildered way, and uttered a few bleats of surprise. The door swung open again, and there on the threshold stood the Duke of Oxenden. He strolled languidly in and laid his hat and cane on the table.

His harsh aristocratic features softened slightly as the pale-yellow eyes took in the scene. Then he perched himself on the desk and, without taking his eyes from Daisy, he said in a hesitant, light voice, "I am sorry I am a little late in presenting the Countess's apologies."

"Apologies!" exclaimed Miss Meaken faintly.

"Yes, indeed," he went on smoothly. "Her ladyship was suffering from the deuce of a migraine yesterday. She begs me to convey her apologies for the hasty letter she wrote you. Her ladyship wishes me to say that both girls were very prettily behaved and a credit to your school and begs that no disciplinary action be taken against them."

Miss Meaken rose to her feet, her short-sighted eyes blinking their relief and amazement. "Well, I must say, Your Grace, that it's very handsome of her ladyship. Very handsome indeed! Daisy Jenkins is one of my best pupils and is shortly to finish her schooling. I would not have liked to see her leave before the end of the term.

"Come girls. Make your best curtsies to His Grace and return to your classroom."

From a sobbing wreck, Amy had become positively radiant. She swept her best curtsy and bestowed her best smile on the unmoved Duke who still watched Daisy.

Daisy had reached the door when she heard his voice calling her, "Tell me, Miss Daisy Jenkins.

Does the name Chatterton mean anything to you?"

Daisy shook her head and then stared at her aunt. For as long as she could remember, Daisy could not recollect her aunt's face as being anything but scarlet. But now it was paper white.

"No!" shouted her aunt. "Never! Chatterton! No! Never!"

The Duke gave Daisy a slight bow and she left the room with her head in a whirl. The mystery of her aunt's violent reaction to the name Chatterton soon fled before the glad thought that the Countess was as kind as she was beautiful. It was only what the Earl deserved. In fact she was so happy with this thought, that the mild Daisy became almost snappish with Amy for suggesting that the Countess knew nothing of the Duke's visit. Amy laughed, "Mark my words, Daisy Jenkins, His Grace is sweet on you. Never took his eyes off you."

"But he's too old!" protested Daisy.

"Old! He's only about thirty. And ever so good-looking."

Daisy looked at her friend in surprise. She thought the Duke looked hard and cruel and that his elegance was positively inhuman. How on earth could anyone consider the Duke handsome compared to the Earl?

The end of the school day arrived all too soon. Daisy could not imagine her stern aunt letting her get away without any punishment whatsoever. She walked slowly homeward, stopping occasionally to answer the questions of the smaller schoolgirls. "No, the Duke had not been wearing a robe. No, he had not been wearing a crown. Yes, he was very handsome," she said, to make up for the disappointment that the Duke had arrived dressed in an ordinary suit of clothes.

As usual Aunt Sarah was waiting on the doorstep, complete with knitting needles. But instead of the usual stabs, Daisy was summoned into the parlor where, wonder upon wonder, a small fire was burning, its meager flames struggling against the surrounding gloom of heavy overstuffed Victorian furniture, stuffed birds, and marble statuary.

"Sit down, Daisy," said Aunt Sarah, not unkindly. She herself sat ramrod straight on the very edge of a high wing chair as if to lean back would encourage Satan himself to snatch her back into the red-velvet depths of the upholstery.

"It is time to talk to you about—*men*," said Aunt Sarah importantly. "We shall say no more about the disgraceful behavior of trespassing on the Countess's property, since my lady herself has seen fit to forgive you. And I was never one to question the ways of my betters."

Daisy remembered many of her aunt's criticisms of the sinful aristocracy, but prudently remained silent.

"I noticed however that His Grace noticed you particular-like. Now when an aristocratic gentleman looks like that, he is not thinking of love or marriage."

"What is he thinking of, Auntie?"

"Lust!"

"Oh," sighed Daisy.

"So I have decided that the time has come to tell you the facts of life. Do you know what a man does with a woman?"

"Well . . . he kisses her and . . . and . . . he says he loves her . . ."

"Codswallop!" said Sarah Jenkins, her face deepening to purple. "Now you listen closely, my girl, and I'll tell you. . . ."

She leaned forward in the firelight, her voice dropping to an intense whisper, and began to outline the mysteries of sexual intercourse.

Daisy stared at her, her wide brown eyes growing enormous with bewilderment. As far as she could make out, the gentleman took his mumble, and mumble, mumble, mumbled with it.

"There!" said Sarah Jenkins. "Now you know. I fear I've shocked you but I am a Christian woman and it is my duty to tell you these unpleasant things for your own good."

Daisy was none the wiser and not much worried. Her aunt could make just reading a novel appear to be some terribly sinful act, so whatever the gentlemen got up to was probably something innocuous. All Daisy wanted to do was to escape to the privacy of her room and dream about the Earl.

But her aunt's whisperings had awakened something in her mind and that night, as she unhooked her Liberty bodice, she looked in the mirror and tried to see herself with the eyes of a sophisticated man. Wide, soft, fawnlike eyes stared back at her, a soft, well-shaped mouth, a soft chin, and masses of soft brown hair.

I'm all soft, thought Daisy sadly, remembering the hard *l*-shaped line of the Countess's jaw. *Colorless—that's what. I wonder what Auntie plans to do with me when school finishes?*

But winter passed, then spring, then came summer and the end of school days, and still Miss Jenkins had not suggested that Daisy earn her bread.

Daisy had been asked to play Juliet in the end of term play to Amy's busty Romeo, but on the subject of playacting, Sarah Jenkins stood firm. It was sinful, it was wicked, and Daisy was to have no part of it. Instead she would attend the methodist chapel that very evening in order to improve the dangerously low tone of her mind.

Nearly in tears, Daisy fled to her room to get ready for church. For once, it had seemed, she was to have a little glamour and excitement. She *knew* she played the part of Juliet well and now it would be played by Clarrie Johnson who roared her lines as if the audience were all stone-deaf. With a jerk, Daisy raised the heavy window of her bedroom and stared across the town with unseeing eyes.

The gardens rioted in all the summer glory of roses. There were red and white roses tumbling over trellises, roses in the hedgerows, and cultivated beauties holding up their heads in the formal gardens like so many ladies at Ascot with their heavy, elaborate hats. The air was heavy with their languorous scent; disturbing and moving. Unbidden, a picture of the house party on the lawn of the castle flashed across her brain. The characters moved with silent grace across the lawns of her mind and the Earl's eyes flashed as blue as the summer sky. With a heavy sigh she turned from the window.

She hauled out her heavy stays from the drawer and examined a tear in the material where a vicious piece of whalebone was poking through. There would be no time to mend it. Well, what did it matter if it dug into her, what did it matter if it were uncomfortable?

She dressed and went downstairs to where her aunt was waiting, encased in black bombazine with multiple jet ornaments that glittered with reptilian brilliance in the dark hall.

Taking her aunt's bony arm, Daisy moved toward the chapel, numb with misery. She felt as if she and her aunt were encased in an impregnable black cloud that no sounds or scents of summer could ever penetrate.

The sermon was to be given by a visiting preacher and her aunt, she knew, was looking forward to the occasion with all the excitement with which London society awaited the first notes of a visiting diva.

By the time they reached the redbrick chapel, her aunt was leaning heavily on Daisy's arm, and for the first time, Daisy felt a pang of concern. Her aunt's face was so red it shone like a beacon.

"Are you all right, Auntie?"

"Yes, of course," her aunt wheezed. "A little short of breath. I will be all right when I sit down."

Sarah Jenkins paused on the porch and turned to the girl at her side. "You know," she said in a rush, "I do *care* for you, Daisy. Worry over you makes me a bit strict. I do care, Daisy."

Daisy looked at her aunt in puzzled embarrassment and searched for a reply, but her aunt was already marching ahead into the chapel. Daisy followed and sat primly next to her on the hard wooden bench.

The preacher was young and intense and was burnt up with the sins of Upper Featherington. The catholic church, he said with a dramatic shudder, had been running a raffle. The prize was a box of groceries. It had come to his ears that not only had members of this congregation taken part in this Devil's lottery, but that one of them had actually *won*. Gasps and cries of consternation arose from the congregation, while heads twisted trying to seek out the sinner.

Gambling, he said, was the sport of Satan. "Amen!" breathed Sarah Jenkins twisting her head to stare at Daisy. Daisy wriggled uncomfortably, feeling that nasty bit of loose whalebone beginning to spear her armpit. Why was auntie staring at her so intensely? *She* had not bought a raffle ticket . . . much as she had wanted to.

The preacher's voice droned on. "A simple thing like a raffle can breed the devilish seed. First it is a box of groceries, then the gambling tables at Monte Carlo."

"Hallelujah!" cried Sarah Jenkins, her jet ornaments flashing in the gaslight.

Delighted with the fervent response, the preacher warmed to his subject.

"Men forsake their wives and families and their children are cast into the gutter. And why? Because the evil vice of gambling has them in its grip. Because . . ."

He broke off. Sarah Jenkins was on her feet, choking and gesticulating wildly.

"It's true," she yelled. "All true. And the righteous have to care for their children and feed them—and—and—"

With a choked moan, she toppled over the pew in front of her, head down. Her ancient elastic-sided boots waved feebly in the air and then were still.

There was silence. Then a long indrawn breath like a sigh, from the congregation. As they gathered around in silence and pulled Sarah Jenkins upright, it was all too evident that Death himself had stalked into the sacred confines of the chapel to claim Sarah Jenkins's soul.

Kindly hands led Daisy from the church. She was aware of the comforting bulk of Curzon, the butler, helping her out into the open air. With a broken little cry, Daisy fell into his arms.

"Why did she have to say she cared for me?" cried poor Daisy with all the selfishness of youth. "Then I wouldn't have cared so much. . . ."

The three days before the funeral passed like a dream. There were constant callers at The Pines from morning till night, constant help, constant advice. And Daisy, as pliable and meek as ever, did exactly what she was told while the corpse of her aunt lay stretched out in the parlor. She numbly went through the ritual of taking in friends and neighbors to "see her," lifting up the lace doily from the now waxen face and standing mutely to attention while the visitors stared and commented.

Curzon had gone through her aunt's meager collection of papers to discover Sarah Jenkins's will in which she left everything she had possessed to "my dearest ward, Daisy."

"This might create a few difficulties," said Curzon, lifting his heavy eyebrows in surprise. "But someone from your aunt's lawyers is to call. And a very classy set of lawyers she has, too. Same as the Earl's. Why now does she refer to you as her ward?"

Daisy shook her head. She had accepted the fact that Sarah Jenkins was her aunt without question.

The doorbell gave an imperious clang and Curzon got to his feet. "That'll be the lawyers now, Daisy. Would you like me to stay?"

"Oh, yes *please*, Curzon," said Daisy, thankful for a familiar face in a world which seemed to be becoming rootless and strange.

The gentleman who entered the hallway with a brisk step did not seem at all like Daisy's idea of a lawyer. He was a fashionably dressed young man with a breezy manner and clever little eyes like boot buttons winking in a chubby, polished face. He sported two magnificent waistcoats and a small diamond pin winked impudently from his stock.

His first words fell like a thunderclap on the startled ears of Daisy and Curzon. He surveyed Daisy up and down with a cheeky grin and then said, "So this is the Honorable Daisy Chatterton. Well, I must say, you don't look a bit like his lordship. Must favor your mother."

Chapter Three

God would surely strike her dead for twittering with excitement on the day that Sarah Jenkins was laid to rest. But the change in Daisy's world had bedazzled her so much that she could scarcely think straight.

She was indeed the Honorable Daisy Chatterton. Her father, Lord Chatterton, was alive and well and living in the South of France. Her mother, Emily, had died giving birth to her and her father had left her in the care of a retired upstairs maid, Sarah Jenkins.

The lawyers had received a letter from her father requesting that she be put in the care of the Earl and Countess of Nottenstone until his return. He had written to the Countess to explain the situation.

The door to the magic garden was wide open. Poor Daisy was only human. Her mind fled from the more unsavory aspects of the case—that, for example, her father had failed to supply Sarah

Jenkins with any money for her care and that her education had taken up a good part of the spinster's life's savings. She would see the Earl again, talk to him on equal terms, be a part of that fairy-tale world glimpsed from the bushes and never forgotten.

The carrier was to take her belongings to the Castle, but Daisy elected to walk, to savor the opening of her new life.

Carrying a Gladstone bag with a few of her private possessions and wearing her best gray alpaca gown, Daisy set out to take up residence in her new home.

Amy Pomfret was waiting at the corner of the road. "Don't forget me, Dais', now you're going to join the nobs," said Amy, giving her a quick hug. Daisy hugged her back, but her treacherous mind was already registering that there was something, well . . . blowsy and common about Amy. She could not envisage her in the elegant surroundings of the Castle.

Without a single pang Daisy left her familiar surroundings behind and with a light step, set out on the golden road to Marsden Castle.

The Honorable Daisy Chatterton, oblivious of her shabby appearance, gave a condescending nod to the startled lodge keeper and walked briskly up the Castle drive. She could see it all. The lovely Countess would rush forward and hug her. The Earl would give his beautiful warm smile.

Her room would be elegant with long windows overlooking the Park. Perhaps she would ride. The money from the sale of The Pines would furnish a new wardrobe and she and the Countess would sit in the evenings, their heads together, turning the pages of the fashion journals, while the Earl looked on and laughed indulgently.

The drive turned and there was the Castle, basking in the summer sun. Tinkling voices and tinkling cups echoed on the still air. Daisy was once again making her appearance at teatime.

She took a deep breath, grasped her bag firmly, and moved across the lawn. The women of the house party tacked elegantly back and forth around the tea table like galleons under full sail, with their lace and bows and enormous hats. A housemaid came flying toward Daisy, the streamers of her cap dancing behind her.

"What was you wanting, miss?" Shrewd eyes took in the best alpaca and the worn Gladstone bag.

"I have come to stay," said Daisy haughtily.

"Then you'd better follow me. You've come the wrong way, miss." Without waiting for a reply, the housemaid sailed off, leaving Daisy to trail behind. She led her to a doorway at the side of the Castle and up and up flights of uncarpeted stairs.

"Here's your room," she said opening a door and giving Daisy a little push. "And you'd best get ready and come down to the kitchens. We're shorthanded."

Then she flitted off before Daisy could reply and clattered back down the stairs.

Daisy looked slowly around her. Where was the elegant suite of rooms she had imagined? She was in a bare attic furnished simply with three cot beds and a hooked rug on the floor. The windows were dingy and barred.

It slowly dawned on her that she had been taken for a servant and all her newfound confidence began to ebb.

"I am the Honorable Daisy Chatterton," she repeated over and over again. "My father is a lord. I will go downstairs and introduce myself. Because if I stay here, I will soon find myself waiting at table!"

Straightening her back and grasping her bag, she ran down the stairs and walked once again to the front of the Castle. Ignoring the footman's yell of "Here, where do you think you're going?" Daisy marched straight up to the Countess.

"I," said Daisy in a very loud voice, "am the Honorable Daisy Chatterton."

"Dear God," said Angela, Countess of Nottenstone, faintly. "What on earth is it?" She fluttered her beautiful hands and appealed to the other guests.

The Earl smiled happily at Daisy, winked and then calmly proceeded to eat a large chocolate éclair.

"Chatterton's gel," said one of the young men, replying to the Countess's question. "*You* know. Poor Old Neddie."

"Oh!" said the Countess. "Neddie. Oh, yes, the poor old lamb wrote something about his daughter, didn't he darling?"

The Earl gave a cream-filled grunt from behind his pastry.

"But what on earth happened to your *clothes*?" remarked the Countess sweetly. "Did poor old Neddie gamble your wardrobe away at Monte?"

"Oh, I say. Jolly good, that!" said a pimply young man. "Can just see old Neddie. Raise you one silk gown, what!" He roared with laughter at his own wit as the other guests joined in the joke.

"Put the handbag on *numero cinq* . . ."

"Stockings on the red . . ."

"Heard of *losing* one's shirt, but I say . . ."

"*Rien ne va plus* . . . except a pair of my lady's *stays*. . . ."

"Oh, Jerry, really. Stays . . . how naughty. I believe the poor thing's going to *cry*. Are you going to *cry*?"

Daisy stood in dumb misery surrounded by her laughing tormentors, her large eyes bright with unshed tears. The Earl lazily got to his feet. "Enough!" he cried. "Leave the child alone. Welcome to Marsden Castle. Curzon! I say, Curzon.

Take Miss Chatterton up to the Blue Room, right?"

"Wait a minute, Curzon," said the Countess. "Darling, the Blue Room is one of our *best* and we *are* expecting Oxenden."

"Oxenden would be honored to give Miss Chatterton his bedchamber any day of the week," said a familiar mocking voice. The Duke of Oxenden pushed his way through the chattering group and picked up Daisy's bag. "Lead the way, Curzon," he said languidly. "Miss Chatterton looks tired and God knows, the inane wit I have just heard is enough to tire anyone."

He held out his arm. Daisy put her arm in his with an unconscious natural grace which made the Countess narrow her eyes. As she walked into the Castle, the Countess's tinkling voice followed her. "Well, darling, she'll need to make herself useful you know. Poor relations always do."

The Duke could see that Daisy was almost at breaking point. He murmured soothing platitudes as he led her through the great hall and up the enormous marble staircase after Curzon's stiff back.

"Now here are your rooms, Miss Chatterton," he said. "I feel you have had enough to bear at the moment. But I have just got back from France and I did see your father. Bring her to the library at six and I'll have a talk with her, Curzon."

"Very good, Your Grace," said Curzon woodenly. He threw open the door of the Blue Room and stood aside to let Daisy enter.

The rooms were all that Daisy had dreamt of. Sunlight flooded through the long windows with extravagant disregard for the oriental rugs spread over the polished floors. The rooms were decorated in Wedgwood blue and white. There was a small sitting room and a large bedroom with an enormous cane-backed bed hung with a frivolous canopy of white lace. White lace curtains floated on the gentle breeze and massive bowls of white roses decorated the occasional tables.

Curzon, who had taken Daisy's bag from the Duke, set it down and surveyed her sympathetically. "Would you like me to give you a bit of advice, miss?"

Daisy kept her back turned to him and said in a small, chilly voice, "That will be all, Curzon."

Curzon bowed and then hesitated in the doorway. "I know what you're going through, miss. If ever you need help, you know where to find me." There was no reply and he closed the door quietly behind him.

Daisy sat down on a chair by the window and wept. She wept because people were so cruel and because her newfound pathetic snobbery had caused her to snub Curzon.

She sat there while the yellow sunlight faded to a rich gold. Then the little French clock on the mantel tinkled out five like a mocking echo of the Countess's voice. Her trunks were still lying corded. She sprang to action and began searching through them desperately for something suitable to wear.

There was a faint scratch at the door of her sitting room and Curzon walked in. "Oh, Mr. Curzon, I am so sorry . . ." began Daisy and then her voice trailed away as she noticed a maid standing behind the butler.

"Plumber here will be your maid, miss. She will lay out your dress and arrange your hair." Plumber folded her large hands over her apron and looked about her in disdain.

"Ah . . . a word with you outside, Plumber. Please excuse me, miss," said Curzon drawing the maid outside the room.

There were the brief sounds of a sharp altercation and then the door reopened and a much subdued and respectful maid stood there. Daisy was still too concerned over her own recent bad manners to Curzon to notice the change in the maid. Plumber had, in fact, been threatened with instant dismissal if she showed so much as an inkling of disrespect and, since Curzon was more of a power in her world than the Countess, she was positively falling over herself in an effort to be helpful.

For the next bewildering hour, Daisy learned the expertise of a really good lady's maid. A faded blue silk gown was sent off to the laundry room to reappear half an hour later looking almost like new. Wielding the curling tongs, Plumber unloosened Daisy's long hair from its braids and set to work to put Miss Chatterton's hair up for the first time. Maids bustled in with lotions and scents, pins and pads. The pads were attached to the sides and the top of the head and her masses of heavy brown hair curled up over them. After a diminutive maid had stitched that offending length of whalebone back into its moorings, more pads were tucked into her stays at the bust and hips and her waist was lashed so tight, Daisy thought she would faint.

Another snap of Plumber's magic fingers and a pair of high-heeled evening slippers were conjured up. "Height," said Plumber severely, "is all the thing."

The little clock tinkled six. There was only time for Daisy to catch a glimpse of the tall, beautiful girl that was miraculously herself in the glass, then her fan was put in her hand and Curzon was waiting at the door.

His wooden face creased in a benign smile. "Well, Miss Chatterton, don't we look a picture!"

All poise lost, Daisy flew into his arms. "Oh, Mr. Curzon, I was so horrid to you. How can you forgive me?"

"There, there, lass," said the butler. "We'll have a talk tomorrow. Now don't cry and spoil that lovely face. Come along, His Grace is waiting."

As they approached the library, Curzon whispered, "Don't be put off by his manner, miss. He's one of the best."

Daisy smiled at him mistily and nodded. She was thinking only of the Earl and the fact that Curzon was talking about the Duke of Oxenden did not occur to her.

Curzon threw open the double doors. "The Honorable Daisy Chatterton," he intoned and, holding her new hairstyle high, Daisy entered the room, tottering slightly on the unaccustomed height of the borrowed shoes.

The Duke uncoiled himself from the depths of an armchair and stood silently surveying the girl on the threshold. The library was dim, lit only by one lamp in the corner. Daisy's delicate hourglass figure was silhouetted against the light from the hall, swaying slightly on her high heels. She moved forward into the room and stood timidly, in the center, her large eyes looking questioningly at the Duke.

"I knew your mother," he said abruptly, motioning her to sit down. "She stood just where you are standing. I was just a schoolboy down from Eton but she treated me with grown-up courtesy. She had great charm."

Daisy remained silent and the yellow, heavy-lidded eyes surveyed her curiously. "We met before," he added gently.

Daisy flushed. She had been hoping that this terrifying aristocrat would have forgotten her school girl escapade.

She opened her mouth to thank him for rescuing her and then remembered he had merely been the Countess's messenger and shut it again.

He continued to survey the silent girl. "You did not know of your father until your guardian's death?"

She shook her head.

"He is well," he said slowly. "I saw him last month in the South of France."

"Could you give me his address, Your Grace?" asked Daisy. "I would like to write and . . ."

She stopped as the Duke shook his head. "It would not be any use. He is not a good correspondent and would not reply to your letters. He means to return to England soon."

"Why did he leave? Is his health bad?"

"No, he is in perfect health," replied the Duke.

How could he tell this fragile girl that her father had fled England after he had been found cheating at cards?

"But I don't understand . . ." she began when a footman padded into the room.

"Apologies, Your Grace," he said. "But my lady wishes to see Miss Chatterton immediately."

"Then tell her ladyship that Miss Chatterton is at present engaged," said the Duke acidly, but Daisy was immediately on her feet.

"I *must* go, Your Grace. It would be extremely rude of me to stay when my hostess wants me."

"As you wish," said the Duke indifferently, picking up a book.

"You should have stayed with His Grace," said Curzon as soon as the door was closed. "My lady means mischief."

"Oh, Curzon. I am sure you are mistaken. I'm sure she's really ever so kind."

"Don't say *reelly* and don't say ever so," said Curzon reprovingly. "You'll need to change your speech, miss, or you'll have that lot making fun of you."

Daisy was too preoccupied with this new worry about speech to question him further about the Countess.

The Countess was lying on a daybed wearing a filmy negligee which revealed more of her charms than Daisy or the townsfolk of Upper Featherington would have considered decent. Carefully averting her eyes, Daisy timidly ventured, "You wished to see me, my lady?"

The Countess widened her eyes at the new Daisy. "Turning into a swan already, are we?" she murmured. And then in a stronger tone, "You realize old Neddie is not exactly paying for your keep?"

Daisy hung her head.

"Exactly. So that makes you a kind of poor relation. And poor relations must help out, mustn't they? Cut my toenails!"

"Pardon?" queried Daisy faintly.

"Are you deaf? I said to cut my toenails. There are the scissors and here is the foot. Understand?" The Countess's eyes were alight with malice.

Daisy could see no way out. She took up the proffered scissors and gingerly took hold of the Countess's foot.

"What clammy little schoolgirl hands you have," sneered the Countess. "And they're *red* . . . just as red as your little nose is getting at the moment." She suddenly kicked the kneeling Daisy on the chest and sent her flying across the room. "You cut me!" she screamed, her eyes dancing with spite.

"What the hell is going on here?" roared a masculine voice as the Earl strode into the room. "Up to your tricks again, Angela? You are to leave Daisy alone, d'you hear me? This is her home and she will stay as an honored guest.

"Now come, my dear." He put an arm around Daisy and lifted her gently to her feet. "Let me take you down to dinner. Little drink beforehand's just what you need, eh?"

Daisy gazed worshipfully into his blue eyes. It was like drowning in a warm blue sea. She could feel the strength of his arm around her tiny waist and his heady masculine smell of bay rum and cigars.

"Oh, have some Madeira m'dear," sneered the Countess. "Honestly, if you had mustachios, you'd twirl them."

The Earl slammed the door on her furious face. "Old cat," he laughed with his arm still around Daisy. "Let's forget about her."

Daisy laughed back, overcome with the heady

excitement of having the Earl's arm around her and hearing the elegant Countess described in such rude terms.

They entered the drawing room arm in arm. "Hey, you yobs!" roared the Earl. "What d'ye think of our little schoolgirl now?"

They all clustered around showering her with compliments as easily as they had showered her with insults. *They're like . . . like jellyfish,* thought Daisy sadly. She had a sudden longing for the plain, honest, middle-class faces of the townspeople and their strong, sensible likes and dislikes. At least one knew where one stood.

But the Earl had decided to be her escort for the evening and under his laughter and teasing, Daisy began to blossom. She was a good actress and carefully copied the accents she heard around her. The evening floated past, mostly taken up by an enormous dinner of bewildering and exotic dishes.

Daisy's head was reeling with the unaccustomed wine and unaccustomed flattery. Much to her shock, the forbidden game of baccarat was played after dinner and she felt too fuzzy to take in remarks about "A Chatterton actually *not* gambling."

Then at two in the morning the whiskey and sodas were brought in with the chicken sandwiches, and Daisy realized she would soon be able to escape to bed.

She slowly edged toward the door and slipped into the hallway.

"Daisy Chatterton!"

A little whisper followed her as she gained the bottom step. She turned her head and her heart gave an uncomfortable lurch as she saw the Earl grinning mischievously. "Let's run away, Daisy. Cackling, stupid lot. I'll show you the gardens."

Daisy looked at him with stars in her eyes and nodded. He took her arm in a comfortable grip and strolled with her out into the scented night. They crossed the moonlit lawns in silence and then the Earl stopped and turned to her.

"You know, I shouldn't be out here with you, Daisy. But you're such a terribly pretty girl."

"But your wife is so beautiful," breathed Daisy in surprise.

"She's a witch!" he said savagely. "If only I could have met someone like you. Sweet and honest."

Daisy drew back. "My lord! You go too far."

"Much too far," said a lazy voice behind them.

"What are you snoopin' round the bushes for, Oxenden?" snapped the Earl.

The black and silver shadows hid the Duke's face, but his voice was hard and cold. "I promised Miss Chatterton's father to keep an eye on her. You should know better, my dear David, than to attempt to seduce schoolgirls in the shrubbery."

The Earl's face went white with anger. "My intentions toward Miss Chatterton are wholly honorable." His head was thrown back in the moonlight, giving Daisy the full benefit of his chiseled profile. She thought her heart would break with sheer happiness. The man of her dreams loved her! He was not afraid to say so in front of this sneering, cold Duke.

The Earl turned and took Daisy's hands in his. "We will speak of this later, my dear," he said in a husky voice. He bent and kissed her gloved wrists one after the other.

Daisy fled across the enchanted lawns and up to the safety of her room, where she twirled around and around, trying to dance away some of the suffocating feeling of delight. He loved her! He would get a divorce. She stopped and bit her lip. Divorce was a wicked word, but this rarified strata of society did not seem to have the same rigid morals as the society that she had left. Why, only tonight she had been introduced to someone's *mistress*! She gave a mock sophisticated shrug and went to bed feeling intensely happy and deliciously powerful and wicked.

The morning brought heavy rain and a bad start to the day. The Countess's personal maid arrived with a basket of her ladyship's underclothes, with a curt note to the effect that Daisy was to mend them immediately.

Daisy's mercurial spirits took a plunge. The wine-induced ecstasy of the night before had disappeared, leaving her feeling small, frightened, and grubby.

"Lust!" cried the stern ghost of Sarah Jenkins in her ear. "Sinner!" wailed the great trees outside as they tossed their arms up to the storm-torn sky.

With a sigh, Daisy decided to forego breakfast and set herself to darning and mending the exquisite lacy garments in the workbasket.

Surely the Earl would come for her. He would take away the degrading work and lead Cinderella from her prison. But it was the solid figure of Curzon who eventually appeared and firmly took the workbasket from her.

"I am sure my lady was mistaken," was all he would say. "Please go downstairs, miss. They have their breakfast about eleven, you know. You won't be late."

Daisy's spirits soared. So that was why her love had not come to rescue her. Curzon sent along Plumber to perform her magic with the curling tongs and the services of the laundry room and then Daisy scampered downstairs in her refurbished button boots.

The breakfast room was crowded with guests, all helping themselves liberally from a staggering assortment of dishes on the sideboard.

The Countess sat at the head of the table, one grilled kidney halfway to her mouth as Daisy entered the room.

"Have you finished my mending, Miss Chatterton?"

"No, my lady," said Daisy, suddenly frightened. "Curzon took it away."

Her ladyship's eyes narrowed as she surveyed the butler's impassive back as he put fresh dishes on the sideboard.

"You're fired, Curzon," hissed the Countess.

"You're hired, Curzon," remarked the Earl amiably.

"Fired!" screamed the Countess.

"Hired," said the Earl, lazily refilling his plate.

"Fired, fired, fired!" said the Countess, throwing her plate of kidneys at the window. The plate bounced off the glass and fell harmlessly to the floor where several dogs sprang to life and squabbled noisily over the meat.

The Countess began to cry pathetically and was immediately surrounded by several young men who patted her hands and called the indifferent Earl a beast. Daisy fled from the breakfast room and took refuge in the conservatory. Her head was pounding. She could *not* go on living in this atmosphere. She had never been aware that she possessed any violent feelings before, but now she seemed to be burning up with hate for the spiteful Countess.

Chapter Four

A faint click as the glass door opened behind her made her turn.

The Earl stood on the threshold looking self-conscious. "You musn't mind about Angela's scenes, my dear," he said, moving forward. "She's a spoiled brat. Always has been. Now, about us. . . ." He moved closer to her, his wonderful blue eyes shining down into hers. Daisy began to feel dizzy and faint. He slowly put his large hands on her waist and drew her close to him.

But seventeen years of middle-class upbringing had left their mark. Daisy drew back abruptly. "This is all wrong, my lord. You are a married man."

All laughter fled from his eyes. "You are right, my dear," he said softly. "I am a bounder and a cad. Only fit to kiss the hem of your dress." He dropped to one knee and suited his action to his words.

Daisy stretched out a shaking hand to the fair

head bent before her, and then with a strangled sob, ran headlong from the room.

The wind shrieked around the castle and the rain pounded against the windows as she fled upstairs and along the corridors, trying to find a place to hide to marshal her jumbled thoughts. She leaned her head against one of the bedroom doors and congratulated herself sadly for having rejected the most wonderful man she had ever met or was ever likely to meet.

"Oh, Jerry!" sighed a woman's voice from the other side of the door. Daisy paused.

Jerry? Then she remembered one of the house guests was a Captain Gerald Braithwaite, dark and handsome in a predatory way. She was about to hurry away when the next sentence halted her in her tracks.

"For God's Sake, Angela, why don't you come away with me and leave that thick-headed clot!"

Daisy stood transfixed. The Countess was in Gerald Braithwaite's bedroom.

"Oh, darling," replied the now familiar tinkling voice. "I would run away with you *tomorrow*. Honestly. I am absolutely head over heels in love with you, you handsome brute. But poor old David's heart would simply break."

Daisy did not wait to hear any more. She walked determinedly to her own rooms and sat by the window, staring unseeingly out at the storm. There was nothing to stop her now. Both the Earl and the Countess were trapped in a distasteful marriage, and the Earl obviously did not know that the Countess would be heartily glad to be free from him. And was divorce so bad? One could not enter the Royal Box at Ascot and minor things like that. And there were no children. In the romances that Daisy loved to read the heroines were always "fighting for their true love." Then she would fight!

The rest of the day passed like a brightly colored dream as the guests played charades and billiards and paper games and cards to relieve the monotony of a country house on a wet summer's day. They passed before Daisy's enchanted eyes in a blur and only one loved face stood out clearly—the Earl's.

How very young all the others seemed to Daisy as they romped and laughed and played inane practical jokes on each other. It seemed to her as if she and the Earl stood alone on a great height looking down at the little people disporting themselves a long way beneath. Oblivious of the Countess's darting glances, she flirted awkwardly with the Earl, drank more than was good for her, and eventually toppled headlong into bed at three in the morning, her head fuzzy and her heart singing with happiness.

The blazing sunlight of a perfect English summer's day woke her early. She was too happy to stay in bed and dressed hurriedly to escape into the gardens and enjoy her newfound romance.

A heavy ground mist coiled through the old trees in the park, and raindrops sparkled like diamonds on the flowers and grass. Somewhere far above a lark sent down its tumbling song, echoing the singing ecstasy in Daisy's young heart.

She sat down on the terrace in a white basket chair, and idly stared out at the beauty of the morning. Then, as if it were meant to happen, the Earl came and sat down beside her. He looked endearingly hesitant and boyish. "Come, my dear," he said, "and I will pick you a rose to match the roses in your cheeks."

Daisy took his arm and they moved to the large rosebushes which grew along the edge of the terrace. The Earl gently turned Daisy around to face him.

"My dear," he began hesitantly. "Can I gather from your looks and words last night that you care for me as much as I care for you?"

Daisy nodded dumbly, too happy to speak. He drew her slowly into his arms and kissed her. The world of castle, lawns, trees, and flowers spun dizzily around Daisy as she returned his embrace with inexperienced fervor.

There was a whistling sound as a heavy object sailed past her ear, and then a tremendous crash of breaking china. The couple broke apart.

The Countess, who had just hurled her best Spode teapot at Daisy, stood at the French windows that opened onto the terrace, her beautiful face contorted with rage.

"You bastard!" she howled.

The Earl's handsome face flamed with anger. "You hellcat," he raged. "It's all right for you to go creepin' along the corridors to Jerry's room, but the minute I try to get a bit for myself, you run amuck."

The Countess dropped her arms to her side with a pathetic gesture. Her hair was loose and she was wearing a lacy wrapper. She suddenly looked very small and vulnerable.

"I only did it to make you jealous, Davy," she said, her voice catching on a sob. "You were making eyes and ogling *her* all the time. I don't care for silly old Jerry one bit."

The Earl looked at her, stunned. "I say, Angela, is that the truth?"

"*Of course*, you great ninny. Can't you see my poor little heart is breaking?"

With a strangled cry the Earl rushed forward and clasped his wife in his arms. "Oh, darling, I was so terribly jealous."

His wife smiled up at him. "Well, it's all right now, isn't it my love. Together again."

"Together," he said fondly, enclosing her in a passionate embrace. Then, still clinging together, they moved slowly off into the castle. Both had forgotten Daisy's very existence.

Daisy stood on the edge of the terrace as if turned to stone. A little breeze had sprung up sending the wreaths of mist flying away raggedly among the trees, like so many ghosts fleeing at cockcrow. The heavy roses nodded, sending little showers of sparkling raindrops onto the terrace. Somewhere high in the morning sky the lark still poured out his exquisite song. The sound of hearty voices started to filter out through the breakfast room windows and Daisy fled. She ran and ran across the lawns and into the trees, panting and stumbling over the underbrush until she was almost at the edge of the estate.

She sank down on a mossy log and doubled up. The pain of rejection and lost love was so bad, it was physical. Then in the back of her mind, she heard Sarah Jenkins's voice—"I do *care* for you Daisy. I do care," and she burst into bitter tears of sorrow and loneliness; a pathetic seventeen-year-old child without a home, adrift on a chilly, heartless, aristocratic sea.

"They always, always go and do it," said a bored voice in front of her. She raised her tear-blurred eyes and found the tall figure of the Duke of Oxenden looking down at her. He sat down beside her on the log and handed her his handkerchief. "Now blow your nose . . . hard . . . that's a good girl. No, I don't want it back. You can sleep with it under your pillow to remind you of your follies."

Anger drove away Daisy's tears. "If you have come here simply to mock and sneer . . ."

"Now, now," he said soothingly. "I came looking for you to see if an explanation would help things. I doubt it. But you do need someone to look after you, my poor child. Oh, don't start sniveling again." Daisy, who had begun to sob at the unexpected kindness in his voice, dried her eyes and sat bolt upright and glared at him.

"That's better," he said bracingly. "Get angry. Get anything. Only don't go under because of the bedroom machinations of that silly pair.

"Now listen to me, my girl. David and Angela have been married for five years during which time they have broken more hearts than you have had hot dinners. They tie some poor youngster into knots and then have a blazing reconciliation and vow never, never to let it happen again. Their short periods of marital bliss last, on average, about six months. And then they both start philandering again."

"But he said he loved me," wailed Daisy. "He said he was only fit to kiss the hem of my gown."

"Well, the latter part was honest at least. Possibly, he did think he loved you. That's what makes David and Angela expert philanderers. For a brief span of time they actually do believe they are in love with the victim."

"The victim," repeated Daisy bitterly. "The aristocracy are supposed to set an example. We were told at school that all lords and ladies were fine and noble."

"Oh, dear," said the Duke. "Well, my dear, the aristocracy is pretty much the same as ever it was. Of course, when the old queen was alive, they were much more discreet, but now Edward is in power, they are kicking up their heels just the way they always did. Under that rigid code of morals and manners beats the heart of a tomcat, my dear."

Daisy hung her head. "If my house isn't sold I shall go back to Upper Featherington."

"And run away," he said gently. "Where's your stiff upper lip?"

"It's over my loose, wobbly lower one," said Daisy with a sudden gleam of humor.

"That's much better," remarked His Grace. "I noticed the way you magically lost your middle-class vowels almost overnight, which means you must be a pretty good actress. So why don't you return with me and pretend that you were merely flirting just as much as David. Angela will be very sweet to you, by the way. They're always extravagantly generous to their victims."

"Oh, how frightfully ripping," said Daisy. "Oh, how terribly, terribly jolly."

She turned and looked fully at the Duke for the first time. He was wearing a hacking jacket and jodhpurs and his long, muscular legs were encased in well-worn riding boots. The harsh, hawklike profile stared into the sylvan setting like a bird of prey. His eyes suddenly slid around to her.

"Feeling better? Hearts don't break, you know."

"Oh, yes they do," said Daisy with spirit. "I feel sick, I have a suffocating pain in my throat and, although I know it is false, I still keep hoping that he loves me."

"Good heavens," said the Duke with lazy

mockery. "All that feeling churning around in such a virginal body. You were not in love, my child. You were simply dazzled by facile good looks, an easy manner . . . and a title."

"Titles mean nothing to me!" snapped Daisy. "You're a Duke. That's greater than an Earl. I didn't fall in love with you."

"I didn't try to make you do so," he said lazily, sliding down to the ground and leaning his head against the log. He closed his eyes.

"*You* didn't try to make me do so," repeated Daisy with a startlingly fair imitation of His Grace's aristocratic drawl. "Let me tell you that I would never fall in love with you. Why—you—you could try till you were blue in the face!"

"Don't be too sure," mocked the lazy voice, as the Duke settled himself back comfortably against the log.

"Have you never been in love?" asked Daisy curiously.

"Never," he replied. "I leave that doubtful emotion to fools and poets. Love! What utter bosh. Love is nothing but a trick of the mind to make a baser emotion more respectable; greed, passion, or where the one wants a daddy to hide her from the naughty world and the other a mummy. Men of my class finally marry because they wish for heirs. They choose a girl of suitable fortune and birth, and if they're damned dishonest or just plain silly or . . ."—here one yellow eye opened and stared at Daisy— "read too many romances, they persuade themselves they are in love."

"Oh, you're insufferable!" cried Daisy, jumping to her feet. "I may have made a mistake with the Earl, but let me tell you I feel in my bones that true love does exist and I—I'll *prove* it to you!"

"Dear me!" He opened both eyes in mock alarm. "Don't tell me you are going to swoon around in front of me with a lot of young men just to persuade me?"

"No. But you will recognize it when you see it. And I will not settle for less, Your Grace."

"You may call me Toby."

"Toby? That's a name for jugs and collies."

"Don't be impertinent. My name is Tobias, the diminutive is Toby. Jugs, indeed! I will place a bet with you, my dear."

"A bet? I have no money."

"A lock of your pretty hair will suffice. Now, isn't that romantic? I, in return, will give you one thousand golden guineas if you can prove to me that you have found the perfect love match. Prepare to lose your hair. Like the rest of us you will settle for money or companionship."

Daisy held out her small, still work-roughened hand. He shook it solemnly and then settled back against the log and closed his eyes.

After a little while Daisy asked timidly, "Did the Earl behave to previous young ladies the . . . the way he behaved to me?"

No reply. She looked down and found to her

exasperation that her noble companion had fallen fast asleep. She took a step forward and then sat down again. In the argument with the Duke, she had, for a few precious minutes, forgotten her hurt. She felt suddenly too frightened to face the house party alone. His Grace had at least given her a role to play to hide her wounds. She looked thoughtfully down at the sleeping figure. What an odd, uncomfortable man he was to be sure. But at the moment he seemed to be her only protector in a strange world. She decided to wait until he awoke.

The couple stayed motionless throughout the long day, the Duke silently asleep and Daisy bolt upright on her log, nursing her pain and feeling a slow, burning anger against her hosts beginning to take its place.

The long light was slanting through the trees and Daisy was just beginning to feel cold and stiff when the Duke awoke. He glanced at the heavy gold Hunter in his waistcoat pocket and then leapt to his feet. "My poor girl! I must have slept all day. I got to my rooms late last evening and then spent the rest of the night reading." He stretched and gave a cavernous yawn. "Poor Daisy, you must be famished. We shall creep round to the kitchens and forage what has been left over from tea.

"Forward then! Daisy Chatterton starts her search for love."

He chatted away, seeming in excellent spirts and

Daisy envied him from the bottom of her heart. She wondered if she would ever feel carefree again.

She hesitated a moment and turned and looked back at the log.

"Have you left something behind?" asked the Duke.

"My childhood," said Daisy sadly.

"But not your dreams," he teased.

"No," said Daisy slowly, "not my dreams."

The couple caused a great flutter in the kitchens when they strolled in demanding tea—or rather His Grace was demanding tea while Daisy hung back in his shadow. "I don't think I shall ever acquire an aristocratic manner," she murmured to the Duke, "if it means putting a great army of servants to a lot of inconvenience."

"Nonsense," he remarked, perched on the edge of the kitchen table. "They love it. Highlight of their day. That right, Curzon?"

"Indeed yes, Your Grace," said Curzon smoothly, adjusting his striped waistcoat. "A great event. We shall talk about it when we go home on our yearly visit to our little country hovels."

Daisy looked at the Duke in alarm, unable to believe that he would let this piece of impertinence go unnoticed. But he only laughed and said, "Damned radical, Curzon. You've known me too long. I suppose what you mean is that we are being a damned nuisance. Come along, Daisy. Drink your tea like a good girl."

Curzon, who looked hopefully at the pair when

they had come in, dropped his eyes in disappointment. His Grace's manner toward Miss Chatterton was fatherly to say the least.

As they were leaving Curzon coughed politely. "Perhaps if Your Grace could spare me a few moments of your valuable time. . . ?"

" 'Course. Run along, Daisy. I'll see you in the drawing room with the rest of the zoo at seven."

When Daisy had left, Curzon dropped his customary wooden manner. "It's like this, Your Grace. Now, joking apart, you know I'm not a one to take liberties. I've known Miss Daisy since she was a babe, her being a member of our methodist chapel."

"No, I don't know Curzon. Methodist, eh! That explains a lot."

"It explains why Miss Daisy has turned out a pleasant-spoken, God-fearing girl," said Curzon sharply.

"Well, out with it man. You didn't waylay me just to read me a sermon. No. I can see something else in those beady little eyes. Philandering in high places. That's what's got you."

"Exactly, Your Grace."

"Well, she's been hurt badly, Curzon, but she's got a lot of character. She's a nice stepper and won't charge her fences."

"Very sound in wind and limb," said Curzon dryly. "We are not talking of a filly, Your Grace, but of a highly sensitive girl. I feel perhaps if I could employ a maid for her—one of her old friends—it might cheer her up."

"Won't that be a trifle difficult? She can't really go around being chummy with her maid."

"The girl I had in mind, Your Grace, would understand that, although she could be friendly with Miss Chatterton in private, but would need to be a correct lady's maid in public. The girl I had in mind is a certain Amy Pomfret."

"Oh, I remember. The dazzling blonde. Well, fix it up, Curzon, and warn this Amy about the Earl's susceptibilities."

"Very good, Your Grace. There is of course a question of salary. . . ?"

"In other words, my lady won't fork out. Tell everyone that Miss Chatterton's father is paying for it. In fact—this is damned embarrassing, but in for a penny in for a pound—I'll get my man of business to send Miss Chatterton an allowance through you as an old family retainer and all that. Tell Miss Chatterton it's from dad."

"But won't Lord Chatterton, so to speak, spill the beans, Your Grace?"

"Not a hope. That old wastrel won't dare show his face this side of the English Channel and he don't care two pins for the girl."

"Very good, Your Grace."

"Well, man. What's up now? Oh, I see. Relax, dear boy. My intentions are as close to indifferent as makes no difference. I have so many pensioners on my books, one more won't make much difference."

Curzon's face broke out into a delighted smile. "Then perhaps, if I may, I will go upstairs and tell Miss Daisy the news."

"Go, by all means," said the Duke vaguely, already dismissing the matter from his mind.

Daisy stared at Curzon with surprise and delight. She was to have money, she was to have Amy. Already in her mind's eye, she saw herself magnificently dressed and the fickle Earl sighing after her with regret.

"Amy can't start right away, miss," said Curzon repressively. "She'll need to be trained first."

But nothing could dampen Daisy's flying spirits. "And my poor, dear father. And to think that all this time I have been thinking that he didn't care for me. I must write to him right away."

Curzon sent up a private prayer for forgiveness. "Your father left instructions, miss, for you not to write. He is a bad correspondent, he says, and any thanks would just embarrass him."

"Oh, well." Daisy's face fell and then brightened. "But it is marvelous, Mr. Curzon, to find a father, so to speak."

"Quite," said Curzon, his face at its most wooden.

Daisy was left to fidget under Plumber's administrations. At last the time had come for her to descend to the drawing room.

It seemed remarkably thin of company. Most of the guests had departed that morning to move to a house party in the next county. Captain Gerald Braithwaite lounged sulkily in a corner by the window, glaring out at the park. An elderly couple, a Mr. and Mrs. Chichester, were trying to interest the Duke in a horse and a faded debutante of indeterminate age fluttered on the edge of their group, making little birdlike jabbings with her nose to emphasize the salient points of the animal in question.

The Countess rose to her feet and ran across the room to Daisy and kissed her on the cheek. "My dear Daisy, another horrid, dreary dress"—and as Daisy stiffened—"now don't go all rigid on me. Such a pretty girl must have some pretty clothes. This is my plan. Come and sit beside me and I'll tell you." She drew Daisy down to sit beside her on the sofa.

"Now, Davy and I have a big surprise for you. We have planned to give you a Season next year. What do you think of that?"

Daisy muttered her thanks and something about now having money of her own, but the Countess swept that irrelevant detail aside. "*I* am going to choose you *the* most marvelous gowns. See—I have the magazines all ready!"

Daisy caught the brooding glance of the Duke of Oxenden, and remembered his cynical words, "They're always extravagantly generous to their victims."

But she sat with her head bent, looking unseeingly at the fashion plates before her and thinking that dreams *did* come true, but in all the wrong ways. Here she was sitting with her head next to the Countess's while the Earl smiled at them indulgently from across the room.

Well, she would play their game and take her Season and become the most beautiful woman in all of London. She would not rest until the fickle, smiling Earl had fallen in love with her. Then she would toss her head and laugh and walk away. The dream was so strong that she did actually toss her head and laugh. The guests looked startled with the exception of the Duke.

She had an uncomfortable feeling that he had just read her mind!

Chapter Five

There was one week to go until the beginning of the London Season, and the servants scurried around the great castle, already preparing for the annual departure to the Earl of Nottenstone's town house.

And Daisy was still in love with the Earl.

All winter long, she had pined and suffered as his careless laugh rang through the castle and his careless hands occasionally patted her on the waist or head, as if she was his pet hound. She had not seen the Duke of Oxenden since the night she had chosen her wardrobe.

Daisy had saved her allowance and bought the Earl a diamond pin for Christmas. He had held the bauble up to the light, laughing and teasing her for being so extravagant, and had then put it aside and forgotten about it with the ease of a spoiled child discarding an expensive but unwanted toy. Curzon had fumed and had threatened to have her allowance stopped. She would have been better employed buying the Duke of Oxenden a present. But when the startled Daisy had stared at him and asked, "Why?" he had been unable to reply.

Amy Pomfret had turned into a highly efficient lady's maid and a constant comfort to Daisy in her struggles to cope with her bewildering new world. Curzon had given Daisy daily lectures on protocol and Amy had supplied her with thumbnail sketches of all the eligible bachelors, gleaned from the gossip of the servants' hall.

The Countess had planned Daisy's coming out ball for the beginning of the Season but, of late, Daisy had noticed that her hostess had been returning to her old snappish ways and was constantly in the company of a Russian Count, Peter Petrovich.

The Count, a restless, dissipated man, seemed to have joined the household permanently, despite the Earl's constant and overt efforts to dislodge him.

One morning shortly before their departure for London, Daisy awoke very early despite her late bedtime of the night before. It had been a horrid evening, she reflected. The Countess had complained all through dinner about the expense of Daisy's Season until that much-goaded girl had told her aristocratic host in no uncertain terms to forget about the whole thing and then had escaped upstairs to have a hearty cry on Amy Pomfret's sympathetic bosom. Daisy was young and feminine enough to want a ball of her very own and to have it snatched from her at the last minute—and because of her own temper—was bitter indeed.

She heard voices below her and crossed to open the window to see who was abroad so early in this nocturnal household. Her heart missed a little beat as she spied the fair hair of the Earl on the terrace below her. Hope sprang eternal and Daisy was about to throw off her wrapper and get dressed so that she could join him and have him to herself for a little, when his voice stopped her.

"Come with me and I will pick a rose to match the roses in your cheeks."

Daisy's hands flew to her own cheeks as all the horror of that sunny morning flooded back into her mind. She walked to the window again. She just had to see who the latest "victim" was. She watched in petrified silence as Amy's blonde curls came into view below her.

"You shouldn't be flirting with me, my lord," Daisy heard her laugh.

"Oh, God, I'm not flirting. Can't you see I'm mad about you?" Daisy winced at the passion in the Earl's voice.

"Well, then," teased Amy. "Give me my rose."

He plucked an early white rose from the edge of the terrace and placed it in Amy's blonde hair. Then he drew the girl close to him and began to kiss her as if he and Amy were the only people in the world.

Bitter tears began to run down Daisy's cheeks.

A loud scream from below echoed around the castle. "Is there no end to this!" screamed the Countess's voice, unconsciously echoing Daisy's thoughts. The couple broke apart. The Earl was scarlet with rage, but Amy seemed remarkably unperturbed. She straightened her lace cap with its frivolous bows and gazed calmly at the enraged Countess.

"Playing fast and loose with the servants . . ." the Countess was screaming.

"And what about that Russian excrescence," boomed the Earl, "shedding pearls and lice, wolfing my food, and seducing my wife?"

"This time you have gone too far . . ."

"*I* have gone too far . . ."

"Lecher!"

"Slut!"

The Countess threw herself at the Earl, raking at his face with her nails. He pushed her savagely away from him and she fell backward onto the terrace.

"Oh, my precious darling, are you hurt?"

"Darling, darling. I'm so sorry. You know I love only you."

"Oh, darling . . ."

"Just a minute!" At the sound of Amy's harsh voice the Earl and Countess stopped their embrace to stare at her. Both seemed immensely surprised that she was still there.

"What about all your promises, my lord?" Amy

went on in a hard voice. "You led me to believe you would marry me."

"*Marry*. You?" The Earl's surprise was so absolute it was almost laughable.

"Yes. Marry," said Amy firmly. "I should have known you lot never keep your promises. You promised poor Miss Chatterton a ball and a Season and then you changed your mind as if it didn't matter. You . . ."

But the Earl and Countess seized on the subject of Daisy's ball as being the least painful matter at hand.

"Of *course* Miss Chatterton shall have her ball . . ."

"Absolutely . . ."

"No question of . . ."

"We shall send out the invitations this very day . . ."

"See that you do," said Amy with pathetic dignity. "One broken heart is enough . . ." She began to cry, staring at the now very embarrassed couple, with the tears welling from her eyes.

Daisy forgot all about her own troubles as her heart ached for her friend. Who knew better than she how the poor girl was suffering?

The voices dropped to a murmur. The three characters in the play moved from view, and then she heard Amy's light step as she ran up the stairs.

Daisy threw open the door, prepared to submerge her own hurt in consoling her friend. But

Amy gave her a dazzling smile and began to pirouette about the room.

She finally sank into an armchair and winked at the astonished Daisy. "Don't look at me like that, Dais'. I did it all deliberate-like."

Daisy could only stare and Amy laughed. "You should just see your face.

"It's like this. His lordship has been making up to me ever since his missus started to play around with the Count. I got a bit worried and told Mr. Curzon. He had warned me about the master. He just said for me to keep out of me lord's way, which I did.

"Then last night I got so upset—what with you crying and saying you couldn't have your ball no more—that I went back to Mr. Curzon. Well, he tells me that my lord and lady always ends up in each other's arms again and they gets very sorry for the persons they've mucked about. So, Mr. Curzon, he tells me to lead his lordship on enough to get my lady mad. Which I did. Which means you've got your ball!"

"But—but—didn't you feel a little bit in love with the Earl?" stammered Daisy. "He is so handsome."

"Naw!" said Amy. "He's just like Jimmy Simpson, the butcher's boy. Jimmy's ever so handsome and he walks out with that plain Margaret Johnson. Well, he keeps letting it be known in little ways to the other girls that he's not quite suited, but after they've made right fools of themselves over him, there he is. Back out walking with Margaret Johnson!"

Daisy felt very young and foolish. How could she have been so bedazzled when her friend seemed not to care in the slightest?

Amy supplied the answer unasked. "I didn't tell you Dais', but I'm promised to Peter, the second footman. Nothing definite, mind. But when you've got a real fellow, I dunno, it sort of protects you from the fakes."

Daisy suddenly remembered her bet. She was more determined than ever to find someone to love and someone who would love her back.

It was some minutes after Amy had left the room before Daisy realized that she had not even thanked her for saving the ball.

In the first few days in London, Daisy felt as if she had just recovered from a long illness. Amy had broken the spell, and every time Daisy looked at the handsome Earl, she was only reminded of Jimmy Simpson. The young men she met began to take on names and faces and recognizable identities, whereas before they had formed a faceless background to the Earl's charm.

She learned from Amy, with some surprise, that the Duke of Oxenden was considered the biggest catch of the Season. She hoped that he would be at her first ball to witness her triumph. Daisy had a new white silk ball gown with a frivolous little bustle and the name tag of a famous Paris house. She had learned that she was attractive. Now all she had to do was fall in love.

On the night of the ball she stood nervously at the top of the long flight of red-carpeted steps. Never had she seen so many jewels. Many of the women wore them in such profusion, it bordered on vulgarity. Who could appreciate the beauty of a fine rope of real pearls when they were worn on top of a diamond necklace? Feathers were considered the last word in chic, and the ladies fluttered into the ballroom like so many birds of paradise. Daisy herself wore a diamond circlet on her brown hair, ornamented with one white ostrich plume, and in her hand she carried a magnificent ostrich feather fan that was so large, she had had to practice for hours beforehand as to how to wield it without knocking over everything in the room.

A heavy undertone of sexuality permeated the ballroom like musk. Daisy had learned from Amy's gossip that the Duke of Oxenden's remarks on the current aristocracy were true. The more raffish elements who had been kept firmly in their places by Queen Victoria, now blossomed as they had never done since the eighteenth century, under the jolly and rumbustious rule of King Edward.

Daisy had long since learned that the whisperings and rustlings in the corridors of a country house during the night were made by the happy guests prowling from bedroom to bedroom. But on the surface, appearances were kept up. Lovers treated each other during the day with all the chilly formality of a Victorian "at home." Public physical contact was forbidden and even the Earl, in this rarified London atmosphere, had ceased to ruffle Daisy's curls or pat her waist.

The Countess indicated to Daisy that it was time to move into the ballroom. Most of the guests had arrived. The Duke of Oxenden had not been among them. Daisy felt a little pang of disappointment.

She moved slowly down the carpeted stairs into the heavy, scented air of the ballroom. The new electricity had been dispensed with for the evening and thousands of candles flickered and blazed from the crystal chandeliers and from tall, ornate, iron stands. Daisy's fragile beauty soon drew a host of admirers and her little dance card was soon full. She studied each face, looking for the man of her dreams. But to her nervous eyes they all looked remarkably alike with their formal black and white evening dress, polished English faces, and high, clipped voices.

Daisy whirled around and around until she began to notice the most determined of her admirers. He was a young man called Freddie Bryce-Cuddestone, who had an endearing boyish face, a mop of fair curls, and large gray eyes. He claimed her hand for the supper dance and was punctilious about finding the right table and seeing that she was immediately served.

After some light social chitchat about various

personalities and wasn't it a *crush* and wasn't it *hot,* Freddie leaned forward. " 'Fraid I'm a bit of an old-fashioned chap, Miss Chatterton. You know, believe in respecting one's parents and all that. How d'you feel?"

"Oh, the same!" cried Daisy, thinking of her newfound, generous father.

"Thought that the minute I set eyes on you. Pretty gel but *good.* Not like some of these rackety types. Pater's dead but I'm very fond of Mater. Lot of the chaps chaff me about it."

"I think it's a commendable feeling," said Daisy stoutly. He looked so young and earnest.

"You know, I really like you awfully. Really, awfully terribly. You don't mind my saying so?"

"Of course not. I think it's very flattering." Daisy felt her heart go out to this decent, amiable young man. Her mind raced on. It would be a comfortable marriage. Their love would grow in a sort of Darby and Joan way. No tremblings of passion, no tears, no hurt.

"Pater was in *tea,*" he said. "But tea's not zactly *trade,* is it."

Daisy shook her head. She had been long enough in her new world to hear people being damned as "being in trade" or "smelling of the shop." But tea and beer were considered respectable.

"Mater, of course, says I shouldn't mention tea because we've got simply pots of money and it's not as if I need to *work* or anything like that."

Daisy experienced a slight qualm which she

resolutely put down. All these young men seemed to drift from club to country house like the butterflies in summer. There always seemed to be a "mater" or aunt or uncle in the background to ensure that these lilies of the field should not have to earn an honest penny.

"We've got an awfully pretty place down at Henley. Love you to see it one day. I say, you don't think I'm being *bold* or anything like that?"

Daisy smiled and shook her head. What a very correct and lovable young man!

He drew his chair closer to hers until their knees were almost touching. "Well . . . you see . . . gosh, this is difficult. Y'see, Miss Chatterton, I'm sort of bowled over in a sort of way. And . . . and . . . I've got this spanking new motor and thought perhaps we might take a toddle down to Henley on Saturday. The Mater would be frightfully bucked. Lonely, you know. Yes, yes. Lonely, that's it. Very solitary. Lonely, yes. Very lonely. All by herself. On her own, you know. Just herself . . . lonely . . ."

Whether from a desire to put an end to the "lonelys" or because she suddenly became aware that the Duke of Oxenden had just walked into the supper room, she was never to know, but Daisy gave an enthusiastic "yes."

"I say," gabbled the delighted Freddie. "Thanks most awfully."

Daisy became aware of the Duke at her elbow and affected the introductions with pretty grace.

The Duke's long fingers reached for her little dance card. "Dear me, Daisy, every single dance taken."

"I've booked the next dance, the one right after supper, Duke. You can have mine if you like," said Freddie generously. "Going to be seeing lots of Miss Chatterton, in any case."

"You are indeed fortunate," said the Duke, looking down at the young pair with an enigmatic stare. "Come, Daisy, the music is starting."

Well aware of many jealous and speculative glances, Daisy moved onto the ballroom floor and into the Duke's arms. He held her very closely and something seemed to happen to her breath, but Daisy decided it was because Amy had been overly zealous in tightening her stays.

"You are not *already* engaged to be married?" Daisy heard him ask.

She shook her head and stared at his waistcoat.

"Then what about that young man who is going to be seeing lots of you?"

Daisy raised her head. "Mr. Bryce-Cuddestone has asked me to go to Henley with him this Saturday to meet his mother," she said proudly.

"What a fast mover for such a shy specimen of English manhood. Don't tell me I am to lose my bet over Freddie Bryce-Cuddestone?"

"And why not?" flashed Daisy. "He is so—so comfortable and *safe* and—and—he doesn't make any remarks to make me feel awkward."

"Is that your recipe for true love?"

"I don't know!" said Daisy, exasperated. "So I'm going to find out. So there!"

But the infuriating man only held her closer. His Grace, the Duke of Oxenden, was not what Daisy would call a comfortable man.

The dance seemed to finish very quickly, however, and Daisy was put into the arms of her next partner, who whirled her around and around with such energy that she felt positively dizzy. When she finally came to a breathless halt and looked around the crowded ballroom, she could see no sign of the Duke's tall figure.

Freddie dutifully called on the Nottenstones the next morning to ask the Countess's permission to take Daisy to Henley on Saturday. He then left, slightly dazzled with the warmth of his reception from the Countess, but, as she confided to the Earl later, the Countess was pleased to see that Daisy had netted an eligible suitor so quickly.

"Old Neddie is not exactly the most respectable of parents," she said. "And then, of course, the girl appears to have no dowry. I must say I am surprised Neddie Chatterton even has enough to give her an allowance. The French casinos must be luckier for him than the English ones."

"Probably still cheating," said her husband dryly.

To Daisy's disappointment Saturday turned out to be a damp, misty day. Beads of moisture gleamed on the shining paint work of the motorcar as she gingerly climbed in and waited for the chauffeur to crank up the engine. She was wearing a new light tweed motoring dress with a motoring hat which the Countess had assured her was the latest thing. It was like a magnified version of a man's tweed cap and swathed in suffocating layers of veiling. After they had putt-putted decorously down the road for a few minutes, Daisy pushed back her veil. The damp air was making it stick uncomfortably to her face.

Henley itself was shrouded in heavy mist as if the town had taken to wearing the latest in motoring veils as well.

It had been a singularly quiet journey and all Daisy's attempts at light conversation had been met with monosyllables. She decided he was nervous.

"Well . . . here we are," burst out her companion finally. "You'll soon meet the mater." He turned and gave Daisy a singularly sweet smile and her spirits rose.

She felt mature and confident. Mrs. Bryce-Cuddestone was sure to like her. Her wedding dress would be of white satin with seed pearls. The bells of London Town would proclaim her married happiness. And the Duke of Oxenden would lose his bet.

Chapter Six

The motorcar swung into the driveway of an imposing Victorian mansion, hidden in a thick grove of trees to screen it from the vulgar gaze. It looked gray, cheerless, and forbidding. Daisy put it down to a trick of the weather.

They were ushered into a chilly drawing room by a cadaverous butler who informed then that he would ascertain whether Mrs. Bryce-Cuddestone was "at home." Daisy looked at Freddie in surprise. Surely his mother was expecting them!

The drawing room reminded her of the parlor at The Pines, only on a larger scale. The mahogany furniture was more massive, the stuffed birds more predatory, and the marble statuary, colder. Heavy red cloths swathed the tables, heavy red cloth draped the mantel, and acid-green velvet screened the offending sight of the legs of an upright piano. A floral Wilton carpet was covered with coconut runner paths at strategic points, and three sets of curtains hid the damp garden from view: heavy red velvet ones on top, lace under those, and muslin ones underneath to trap the last bit of daylight.

A prickly, angular cactus swore at them from the empty fireplace and multiple photographs of various Bryce-Cuddestones glared at them from all points of the room.

There was a smell of dust, potpourri, and Brown Windsor soup.

Daisy was starting to feel irrationally guilty and was just beginning to wonder what on earth she had to feel guilty about, when the door opened and Mrs. Bryce-Cuddestone stood on the threshold.

She was a vast, imposing woman, rather like a figurehead on a tea clipper; all bosom and chin. She was dressed in black silk, ornamented here and there with various cameos of Greek ladies who also had large bosoms and thrusting chins. Her masses of iron-gray hair were set in rigid curls. She had obviously resorted to a mixture of sugar and water to get the effect, for little sugar crystals clung to various iron curls and tendrils like a kind of exotic dandruff.

Her opening words were—as Daisy was soon to find out—typical.

"Oh, my poor, deluded child," she cried, moving majestically toward her son. "Another one?"

"But Miss Chatterton's *different*, Mater," said Freddie earnestly. "She believes in the sanctity of the home and all that."

"Humph!" Mrs. Bryce-Cuddestone folded her

large hands and swiveled her large pale eyes to survey Daisy.

"I should hope so," she boomed. "Ours has always been a happy home. When Reginald was alive,"—here she produced a lilac handkerchief with a black border and held it under her massive nose—"there was nothing but happiness from morning till night."

"I did not know you had been recently bereaved. I am so sorry," said Daisy.

"It was only fifteen years ago when Reginald was taken from me," went on her hostess. "I have been mother and father to that boy. The designing hussies he has brought to this house have been enough to break a mother's heart."

"Oh, I say, Mater!" bleated Freddie, but Daisy was already on her feet.

"I do not like the implication that I am another designing hussy," she said in a high, thin voice. "Mr. Bryce-Cuddestone, I wish to leave."

To her horror, Mrs. Bryce-Cuddestone burst into noisy tears. "I've gone to such trouble, Freddie. I've worked and slaved to have a very special luncheon for you, and now because I have been misunderstood, it will all go to waste."

"Here, I say, Mater. I say, Daisy. I say, look here. Stay for luncheon. Can't have tears. Buck up, Mater. She's stayin'. Ain't you, Daisy?"

Poor Daisy could only nod dumbly. Again she felt guilty and could not quite understand why.

"Luncheon is served," came the tomblike voice

of the butler from the doorway. Freddie held out his arm to his mother and Daisy trailed after them.

The dining room table was long and massive, an eternity of gleaming mahogany. At the halfway point there was a sort of crossroad made with two huge silver salt-and-pepper shakers and a fat silver epergne depicting a young Greek with his clothes being shredded by silver wolves.

Mrs. Bryce-Cuddestone sat at one end, Freddie at the other, and Daisy at the crossroad in the middle. The dining chairs were heavy and squat. Daisy sank down into the cushion of her chair and found that her chin was almost on a level with the table. Freddie and her hostess had similar chairs and they looked as if their heads had been served up at either end.

Conversation had to be carried on at the top of the voice, although, as Daisy reflected, it could hardly be called conversation. An interrogation was more like it. Did Miss Chatterton have a dowry? Was Miss Chatterton aware that the happiest married households had the mother-in-law in residence? Were the Earl and Countess of Nottenstone as rackety as she had been led to believe?

Daisy began to get quietly furious. She felt like a pot on a slow burner, gradually rising to the simmering point, and about to boil over any minute.

The meal was a perfect symphony of starch. A bowl of broth in which some animal had placed a paw, was piled high with potatoes and barley.

Then came a sliver of fish in a whole winter's coat of breadcrumbs. Then a minuscule mutton chop cowering under a mountain of mashed potatoes and butter beans and then a Cabinet pudding which should never have been appointed to any table. The "full-bodied" wine tasted to even Daisy's uneducated palate like vintage yesterday.

Mrs. Bryce-Cuddestone had obviously never heard the social law of not speaking with your mouth full. She talked steadily throughout the meal, posting away great quantities and lecturing Daisy on Freddie's delicate constitution.

Reginald asked me, when he was dying, to send the boy to Eton. Me! Send my son to be mauled by a lot of rough boys! He always had his own tutor here in his beloved home. Are you wearing your flannel underwear, Freddie? We were so happy. Then Freddie ups and breaks my heart and says he is taking diggings in London and is going to find a wife. Did you ever hear of such ingratitude, Miss Chatterton? I could have chosen a nice local girl for him, but he needs to go chasing after flighty society girls."

Mellowed by several glasses of the "full-bodied," Mrs. Bryce-Cuddestone surveyed Daisy across the sea of mahogany. "I must say all the same, you seem like a nice, biddable little thing. Could be molded to the Bryce-Cuddestone manner. Yes. Yes. Could be *formed* as a sculptor forms a figure out of raw clay. I am very artistic." She suddenly let out a cavernous yawn. "You have my permission to show her the garden, Freddie."

Freddie looked like a child at Christmas. "Oh, I say, Mater. That's simply ripping. Come along, Daisy. I may call you Daisy, mayn't I? We're going to see lots of each other."

Daisy's heart sank to her little kid boots. She followed Freddie out into the misty garden. He turned toward her, his face radiant.

"The mater *likes* you. Isn't that marvelous? You must admit it's the greatest compliment you've ever received."

Now Daisy had been taught all her young life to respect her elders, so she bit back the angry reply on her lips. Freddie took her silence for acquiescence and maidenly modesty. "Let's take the old bus out for a spin. I'll drive you myself."

Daisy agreed. The sound of the engine would at least prevent any lengthy conversation. They rattled out onto the road, Freddie in high spirits and Daisy in the depths of misery. What a horrid day it had turned out to be! And she had thought that she simply *had* to pick out a personable young man, marry him, and live happily ever after. She had not envisaged such unromantic obstacles as mothers-in-law.

They had gone a little way out of the town and were chugging along a country road through the thickening mist when Daisy spied three still figures lying beside the road. "Oh, do stop!" She put her hand on Freddie's arm. "Someone's had an accident."

Freddie stopped and looked over his shoulder. "I wouldn't worry about that," he said. "Let's go on."

Daisy looked at him in amazement. "There are three people just lying beside the road."

"Let them lie," said Freddie, and then sighed heavily. Daisy was already out of the motor and running back along the road.

The three figures, a man, woman, and small child, lay in the thick grass beside the ditch. Beads of mist rimed their hair and their torn and shabby clothes. The woman clutched the tiny child to her emaciated bosom. All three were dead.

With a small whimper Daisy drew back. "What on earth happened?" she sobbed to Freddie, who had come up behind her. He shuffled his feet awkwardly. "Starved to death, I should say. Pretty common, you know. Parish'll come along to pick 'em up. Let's go. You can't do anything for them now."

Daisy walked slowly back to the motorcar. She found that her hands were shaking. "How on earth can people just starve to death in England?"

"They do it all the time," said Freddie cheerfully. "Not around your part of London, of course. Fact is, they're lazy. Simply won't work, you know. Poverty's like a disease. They can't seem to shake it off."

Daisy desperately wanted to believe him. But

the picture of the little child's emaciated, claw-like hand as it had died clutching its mother's coat swam in front of her eyes. "But a little child," she whispered.

"Nasty for you," said Freddie sympathetically. "Put it out of your mind. Better get back soon. Mater'll have had her nap."

Daisy had been mild and meek all her young life, but she was suddenly flooded with such strong hatred for the mater that she thought she would faint. What on earth was happening in the world? She had seen enough food thrown away after a house party to have kept that poor family for a year!

As Freddie parked the motor in the gloomy driveway he whispered, "No need to trouble Mater with our little adventure. She's very sensitive, you know."

Daisy thought privately that Mrs. Bryce-Cuddestone showed all the sensitivity of an over-fed water buffalo and bit her lip.

This time mater was waiting for them in the drawing room, fortifying herself from the sherry decanter. She twinkled at them with a roguishness hideous to behold. "Ah, now what have my two young things been up to?" She wagged a playful finger at them. "Have a glass of sherry, Daisy. I have told the housekeeper to bring the books and we'll go over them together."

"Why?" asked Daisy, made bold by a sudden spasm of fear.

"Why! So that you will learn how to run a mansion such as this, my dear. I am sure you will prove an apt pupil."

Daisy felt the prison walls closing about her.

"I do not think it necessary to go to such trouble since the running of—of your household is no concern of mine," she faltered.

Mrs. Bryce-Cuddestone put down her glass so forcefully that she nearly broke the stem. "My dear girl," she snapped, "I gathered that you had accepted my son's proposal of marriage and since you seemed such a pleasant girl, I decided to overlook your unfortunate family background. Father, you know."

Daisy's eyes filled with tears as she thought of her generous father who faithfully sent her allowance to Curzon every month. She got to her feet. "Your son did not propose and had he done so, I would not have accepted."

"Oh, I say!" bleated Freddie.

"Furthermore," went on Daisy, quite pink with anger, "it is very rude of you to insult my father. I wish to leave. Immediately!"

Mrs. Bryce-Cuddestone's face turned puce then purple. She emitted a few strangled noises and then began to scream and drum her heels on the floor.

"Now look what you've done!" shouted Freddie, ringing the bell like a fire alarm. "Poor Mater."

His boyish features suddenly seemed old and mean. "If you've killed her, then it's your fault."

Mrs. Bryce-Cuddestone had begun to moan. Two burly footmen and a lady's maid rushed into the room and bore the anguished lady out. Freddie and Daisy faced each other in silence as the moans progressed up the stairs and slowly died away.

"I must go," Daisy said in a small voice. Freddie glared at her. "I think you should at least have the decency to stay until Mater recovers. I'll go and tell the housekeeper to prepare your room. And"—as Daisy made a horrified movement to protest—"if you want to leave, you'll need to go by yourself. 'Cause I ain't taking you."

He went out of the room and slammed the door.

Daisy stood stricken, listening to the sounds of his retreating footsteps. A statue of Niobe, all tears, gazed at her sympathetically across the room. She began to search feverishly in her reticule. No money. And even if she had money, she no longer had the courage to venture outside into the ever-thickening mist. She felt like a small animal, trapped in a cage of heavy furniture and stuffed birds.

The Duke of Oxenden strolled up St. James's toward his club, reflecting that the weather was so foul, it might as well be the middle of winter. Yellow acrid fog prowled the gloomy streets, bringing an early night to London. The gas lamps had already been lit and their faint bluish flames were only slightly discernible. He leaned against a lamppost to light a cigar. The mantle of the gas lamp above him had been broken and the light sputtered and hissed and sang its dreary winter melody over his head. A fine rain of soot was beginning to fall and his white cuffs were becoming slowly speckled. He walked on toward his club and pushed open the double glass doors to escape the dismal evening.

But the fog was no respecter of class or persons. It hung over the club room in great yellow bands and dim figures could just be made out, sitting in their armchairs, like survivors from a shipwreck adrift on a yellow sea.

He found an empty armchair and a copy of the *Times,* its pages still crisp and warm from its ironing—one dreadful day the club steward had forgotten to have the members' newspapers ironed and pressed and had nearly lost his job—and settled back.

A familiar face came looming up out of the fog. "Hullo, hullo, hullo," said Lord Harry Trenton cheerfully. "What y'doin'—samplin' the wicked delights of the Season?"

The Duke put down his newspaper and looked affectionately at his friend. Lord Harry Trenton was often pointed out as being a prime example to explode the myth that there is such a thing as aristocratic features. His line dated back to the Norman Conquest and he looked like a coal heaver. He was burly with a red hairy face, a thickset body, and massive hands with broken fingernails.

"Why shouldn't I be here, Harry? Time I was getting married and this is the best market. I may be getting too old, all the same. I've never seen such a dreary bunch of debutantes."

"Oh, I dunno," said Lord Trenton, sinking into the armchair opposite, which gave a loud protesting creak. "Some of 'em ain't so bad. Saw you at the Chatterton gel's ball. Now there's a beauty."

"Miss Chatterton is certainly very pleasant to look at," remarked the Duke dryly. "But much too young. I haven't gone in for cradle snatching yet."

"Well, you probably wouldn't have the chance anyway," remarked his friend cheerfully. "She's gone off with young Bryce-Cuddestone for the day and you know what that means?"

The Duke sat up in his chair. "No, I don't know what that means. Pray tell me."

"Well, it's like this. Freddie Bryce-Cuddestone's got this terrifying mother. He dotes on the ratbag. Kept takin' likely girls to the house and the old harridan would make sure Freddie never saw 'em again. Right? But Freddie's still pursuin' the ladies an' he's livin' in London an' the old rumty-too can't get her hands on him and bully him like she used to. So she ups and tells him that the debs he's bringing around are too *fast* and modern. But *if* he found a sort of sweet old-fashioned gel that she could have the trainin' of . . . well, she'd ring the marriage bells herself!"

"I am sure Miss Chatterton cannot be *forced* into marriage in this day and age."

"Oh, no? You obviously haven't met Freddie's ma. I called round at the Nottenstones to pay my respects and found out where she'd gone *and* that a message had come from Henley to say she was stayin' on a visit and to send her clothes."

The Duke shrugged with irritation. "And you think she's being kept prisoner? All she has to do is just walk out."

Lord Trenton hitched his chair closer.

"Look at it this way. If you was a shy gel and some matron insists you stay and you've never been to Henley so it could be Naples as far as you're concerned, and you ain't got any idea of how to get out of it . . . well . . ."

"Why don't you go and rescue her?"

"Can't," said Harry Trenton, getting to his feet. "I'm squiring my sister to the opera tonight. Damned lot of caterwauling. But I promised. Toodle-oo." He heaved his massive figure out of the chair and disappeared into the fog.

The Duke of Oxenden rattled his newspaper impatiently and turned to a report of the war in South Africa. He remembered Daisy's fragile appearance and timid air and swore under his breath.

Dinner at the mansion in Henley was a gloomy affair—for Daisy at least. Mrs. Bryce-Cuddestone had been dosed with laudanum and her snores reverberated overhead like distant thunder. Daisy had enough good sense to gather that Mrs. Bryce-

Cuddestone's tantrums were of frequent occurrence and to turn a stony face to Freddie's emotional blackmailing. Freddie was implying that since Daisy had put the mater at death's door, the least she could do to make amends was to marry him.

Daisy reflected that she had never been subjected to such expert bullying before. Her clothes had arrived and yet no one had told her she was expected to stay. She could only be thankful that Freddie's puppylike amorous sallies had, for the moment, been kept at bay by the length of the dining table.

The trifle had been removed and Daisy rose to her feet to leave Freddie to his port. But to her horror he rose also, taking the decanter with him. Since there was only the two of them, he said blithely, they should be cozy together in the drawing room. He offered Daisy his arm but she affected not to notice it and moved in front of him across the hall. She refused to acknowledge the arrival of her trunks and had dined in her traveling dress.

This was an England she had never dreamed of, reflected Daisy bitterly, *where innocent people starved to death on the roads and this particular flower of English manhood seemed hell-bent on seduction.* She looked wildly about her for some sort of weapon but everything in the chilly, overstuffed room seemed to weigh a ton.

Both jumped nervously as the doorbell clanged

noisily into the Henley night. Freddie crossed quickly to the door of the drawing room and waylaid the cadaverous butler. "I say, Smeekers, whoever that is, tell 'em we ain't at home."

"Very good, sir," remarked Smeekers with a slow smile. He opened the door and Daisy faintly heard the sound of a familiar voice raised in question and then Smeekers's firm and distinct reply, "I am afraid Miss Chatterton is not at home, Your Grace."

"Oh, yes I am," yelled Daisy, galvanized into action. She sprang past the openmouthed Freddie and hurled herself into the hallway.

Looking like an elegant and friendly demon, the Duke of Oxenden lounged in the doorway. He wore a high silk hat rakishly on the side of his head and a long beaver coat and his yellow eyes gleamed with mischief. "Ah, Miss Chatterton. I have been sent by the Countess to escort you home. You have a heavy day of social engagements tomorrow, she begs me to remind you."

"Oh, th—thank you," stammered Daisy. "Your Grace, they sent for my trunks."

"In that case we'll simply send 'em back," he said languidly. "Come along like a good girl."

"I say," said Freddie sulkily. "There's no need for Daisy to rush off in the middle of the night in all this fog. Dangerous, what!"

"There are more serious dangers around than mere fog," said the Duke looking coldly at Freddie, who blushed. "Here, you," to the butler, "get Miss

Chatterton's trunks corded up and put in my carriage."

To Daisy's bewildered eyes the world had miraculously righted itself. In no time at all her trunks had been strapped on the back of the Duke's carriage and she was making her farewells.

She sat in silence as the horses clopped down the drive, aware of the Duke's eyes on her.

"Well, Daisy," he said at length. "Aren't you going to thank me for rescuing you?"

Pride was about to make Daisy say petulantly that she hadn't wanted to be rescued, but escaping from the Bryce-Cuddestone household was such a relief that she found herself bursting out with the story of her horrible day and the dead bodies beside the road.

He listened sympathetically until she finally finished her account in a hearty burst of tears. "I am afraid there are a lot of people like the Bryce-Cuddestones around. They turn their eyes away from poverty and misery and say that it is all the fault of the poor themselves to ease any pangs of conscience they may feel. Or they get up elaborate charities complete with crested paper and hundreds of overpaid officials so that by the time *they* are paid off, there's precious little for the poor."

"If I could donate something from my allowance . . ." said Daisy. "I am sure my father would not mind."

The Duke regarded her in silence and then said

after a few minutes, "Well, I see no reason why not. I shall give you the name and direction of a vicar in the East End. He does a great deal of *real* charitable work. Your money will not be wasted, I assure you. Now, we shall stop in Henley at the police station and I shall report the matter of your dead bodies."

Daisy blinked back her tears and thanked him profusely. She decided she had been mistaken in him. He was not hard and cold after all. After they had left the police station she began to chatter merrily and, being a good mimic, soon had him laughing over the tantrums of Mrs. Bryce-Cuddestone.

"You see, my dear," he said at last. "It all bears out what I was telling you. True love does not exist and it seems to me as if your search for it is only going to cost you endless agonies. I am prepared to cancel the bet."

"Never!" said Daisy warmly. "I shall prove it to you yet, Your Grace."

"Toby," he reminded her gently.

"Your Grace," snapped Daisy petulantly and then settled back in the carriage and pretended to go to sleep. For some reason she could not fathom, she was almost as angry with the Duke as she had been with Mrs. Bryce-Cuddestone.

"Very well then," said the light mocking voice. "But don't expect me to rescue you next time. . . ."

Chapter Seven

The unchristian fog fled before a light breeze and sparkling sunshine on Sunday morning, leaving its sooty residue in the nooks and crannies of the great city.

London slumbered on under a pale summer sky and only the sparrows were up and about, chirping cheekily on the elegant windowsills of the West End like so many Cockney urchins come to poke fun at the sleepy aristocracy. Daisy lazily opened her eyes and wondered if she had been wise to make any engagements for the day at all. Mrs. Bryce-Cuddestones seemed to be lurking in every corner of fashionable London, ready to drag her off to their gloomy homes and force her to marry one of their downtrodden offspring.

But Lady Mary Trenton had invited her for tea and she was to stay on for dinner. Lady Mary, the coal heaver's sister, was a sturdy, jolly, harmless girl. The most she might suffer from was boredom. Daisy rang the bell and blinked at the strange maid who answered. It was Amy's day off so there was no way of picking up any useful servants' gossip about the Trenton household.

Daisy passed most of her day buried in the Earl's sparse library, lost in the world of Mrs. Henry Wood's novels.

What agonies the heroines had to endure. What smooth villains twirling their mustaches lay in wait for innocent damsels. But virtue triumphed in the end . . . in most cases.

Woe befell the woman who strayed! She lost her children or had to spend the rest of her life in obscure watering places on the Continent, suitably veiled. Daisy reflected cynically that the present society seemed to get away with murder when it came to liaisons and seductions.

But her love was waiting for her just around the corner. She was sure of it. And what better time to meet him than on this sparkling day.

The Trentons had a large Nash town house in Regent's Park. The other guests seemed to be mostly young people, many of whom were already familiar to Daisy. They seemed to laugh a lot and treat everything as a mad kind of joke. Daisy sat down at the tea table in the garden in all the glory of her new tea gown—and leapt to her feet as her seat let out a loud raspberry. Everyone cheered and clapped. A bladder had been placed under her cushion, explained Mary Trenton. Such a gloriously *vulgar* noise. The Trentons like most of London society loved practical jokes and as Daisy nearly broke her teeth on a wooden angel cake, she wondered if she would survive the day.

She became aware of a tall man watching her intently across the room. He had been talking to Lord Trenton and now stood staring at Daisy with such intensity that she blushed and dropped her eyes.

Lord Trenton led him forward to be introduced. He had a square, handsome tanned face, broad shoulders, and was impeccably dressed in a scarlet blazer and white flannels.

He was introduced as a Captain Richard Brothers who was home on leave from India. He had merry, laughing eyes and an endearing smile. Daisy began to feel her heart beating quickly as she smiled up at him.

He pulled up a chair beside her. He neither shouted at her as if she were deaf, nor did he immediately start questioning her about a lot of people she had never heard of, but began to entertain her with thumbnail sketches of the company and then went on smoothly to describe his adventures in India. "It's a great country," he told the dazzled Daisy. "And don't you listen to any of those fools who say it's no place for a lady. Why, the ladies have a marvelous time. Not enough of them, you see. Even the plainest girl has several subalterns at her feet. As for you—we'd all be fighting duels."

He described the blazing stars of the tropical nights, the exotic flowers, the sparkling social life, until Daisy felt ready to rush off and jump on the next boat.

As tea was finished, they were both very pleased with each other. Daisy, because she had never been in the company of such a handsome, brave man. Why, he made the Earl seem positively effeminate!

Captain Brothers was just as enchanted with Daisy. Lord Trenton had described Daisy, in a spirit of schoolboyish mischief, as "London's latest heiress," being well aware that the Captain was a notorious fortune hunter. Lord Trenton was not an unkind man and he determined to set the Captain right as soon as possible—and then forgot about it.

The company retired to their rooms to dress for the evening's pleasures. Daisy felt so happy she could hardly breathe. The Trentons were very fond of amateur theatricals and had asked her to recite something from *Romeo and Juliet.* At last she could play Juliet!

Mary Trenton had said it was not necessary to wear a costume. Her evening gown would do. She would be a very Edwardian Juliet in blue silk and a bustle, but she knew the role by heart and was sure she would do well. And the Captain with the merry eyes would be watching her!

A makeshift stage had been set up in the ballroom at the back of the house. Daisy waited nervously behind the curtains and had a sudden stab of panic. She had chosen the speech Juliet makes before she takes Friar Lawrence's drug. Clutching a bottle of smelling salts to act as a phial, she heard Lord Trenton's jolly voice announcing her. The curtain parted, the candles in the footlights flickered and waved, and then Daisy was quite alone facing her audience.

In a firm clear voice she started to recite, "Farewell. God knows when we shall meet again . . ." and then lost herself in the beauty of the words. She had reached the middle of the speech—"How if when I am laid into the tomb,/I wake before the time that Romeo/Come to redeem me—" when she became horribly aware that her audience was rolling around with laughter.

Her voice faltered and then went on. She had always considered the line "And madly play with my forefathers' joints" slightly ridiculous if taken out of context, but surely it could not merit the gales of noisy mirth. Tears of laughter were running down Lord Trenton's face and he was forcibly holding back Captain Brothers who was trying to leap onto the platform.

Daisy turned slowly around. Two clowns from the Hippodrome, hired specially for the evening, were cavorting behind her as they had been all along. With two spots of color on her cheeks, Daisy swept from the platform and straight out of the house. She had money with her—having learned her lesson at the Bryce-Cuddestones—and flagged down a passing four-wheeler, ignoring the noisy cries of the guests who had chased after her onto the pavement. "Can't you take a joke? I say, no need to scamper off like that . . ." followed her down the road.

Daisy crept miserably to bed, missing Amy desperately. She had just met the man of her dreams and now he probably thought she was just a silly little goose. Then she remembered that the Captain had been trying to stop the performance and felt oddly comforted. Not since she had got over her infatuation for the Earl had Daisy had anyone to dream about until now. She fell asleep at last with the picture of the Captain's face before her eyes.

Angela, Countess of Nottenstone, was extremely angry when she heard, the following day, of Daisy's flight from the Trentons. "Such a *humorless* little girl, Davy," she moaned to her husband. "We really must find her a young man since she doesn't seem able to do it for herself."

The couple were seated over a late breakfast. Lady Trenton had just sent around a long and anguished message that they hadn't meant to be *cruel,* it had all been in a spirit of fun.

"Is Miss Chatterton awake yet?" she asked the hovering Curzon. The butler shook his head. "I do not think so, my lady. Miss Chatterton is still in her room, I gather."

"Sulking," commented Angela, buttering a piece of toast. "If we don't unload her this Season, Davy, she can go and join her father or go back to her methodist chapel or *something*."

Both the Earl and Countess turned around in surprise as Captain Richard Brothers was announced. "Show him in," said Angela, with an elegant wave of her toast. "One of your friends, Davy?"

"Never heard of the chap," said the Earl languidly.

"Perhaps we should tell Curzon to send him away. He may be after *money* . . ." But the handsome Captain was already being announced.

Angela smiled charmingly at his expensive gray suit and at the sunlight twinkling on the gold thread of his waistcoat.

"I called to ask your permission to take Miss Chatterton on an outing," he said. "She confided to me that she had not yet seen very much of London and since I'm just back from India, I would like to see some of it myself." His blue eyes twinkled appreciatively at the Countess who dimpled back, while the Earl looked gloomily into his coffee cup and reconsidered the charms of the new upstairs maid.

"I am sure any girl would be delighted to have such a gallant escort," said the Countess, leaning toward the Captain who was now seated at the table next to her. A waft of her musky perfume twined itself around him and he gazed at her in a bewildered way. Without taking her eyes off him Angela rang the bell and sent the glad tidings of the Captain's arrival upstairs to Daisy's room.

Daisy was still miserably smarting under her

humiliation of the night before. The news of the Captain's arrival by the recently returned Amy broke up her dismal mood. Her heart was fluttering and she felt very young and nervous. Did Amy know anything of the Captain? No, Amy didn't. But if Daisy would only wait a minute she would inquire in the kitchens. But Daisy had a sudden revulsion against listening to servants' gossip. She must trust somebody after all.

In a record length of time, she entered the breakfast room in all the glory of a new pink organza dress with a high-boned collar, leg-o'-mutton sleeves, and a frivolous parasol to match. Her wide picture hat was swathed with pink tulle and prettily shadowed her small face. The Captain broke away from the Countess's spell with a little mental wrench and hastened to her side. Before he took her hand a black cloud composed of tailor's bills, club bills, and the bill for the smart rented brougham outside crossed his mind, but was soon dispelled. This little girl's fortune would soon settle them all.

It had been difficult to make a play for wealthy girls in the small, enclosed society of Ranchipoor, but here, in the bigger marriage market of London, it should be possible to marry some money before his unfortunate reputation followed him home.

Looking the very picture of youth, beauty, and wealth, the couple left the mansion and climbed into the brougham. The coachman cracked the whip and the carriage moved down the street.

They had a magic afternoon as the carriage ambled through the streets and parks of London. Modest as she was, Daisy's head under the pink tulle hat was turned by the admiring looks and comments the pair received.

The Captain was charmed. His large hand lingered a little longer on Daisy's each time he helped her down from the carriage to view a building or a park and Daisy's heart began to beat faster and faster with a strange triumph. This was it! Love at last. She would travel with him to exotic India and break the hearts of every young subaltern in his regiment.

He proposed they finish their day with a trip to Greenwich for dinner. Daisy climbed happily aboard the coaly steamship, pleasurably aware of the admiring glances the women passengers cast at Captain Brothers.

The late afternoon sunshine had transformed the muddy waters of the Thames to molten gold. All the filth and misery of the great city were washed away by the dazzling light and London looked as if it had been newly painted by Canaletto. Heavy coal barges became black and gold gondolas as they slid past, and the bargee's washing, the flags of some Italian state.

The cupola of St. Paul's seemed to hang over the motionless city and the pennants on the Tower stood out stiffly like cardboard. Daisy felt suspended in time, alone in the middle of a golden world with her handsome Captain.

"Richard . . . Richard Brothers!" A shrill female voice at their elbow broke the spell. Daisy suddenly became aware of the chill wind from the river and shivered as she turned around.

A faded, raddled female in her forties stood clutching the arm of a gentleman who could only be described as a masher.

From his insolent, protruding eyes and his curly brimmed bowler, to his flamboyant waistcoat and natty elastic-sided boots, he looked like a stage version of a bounder. The lady was peering anxiously at the Captain over a sort of hedge of puce feather boa. Her painted face creased into a smile of recognition. "It *is* Dickie. Recognize those shoulders anywhere."

The Captain leaned against the rail and surveyed the pair. "I am afraid I haven't had the pleasure . . ."

The woman's eyes narrowed. " 'Course you have, love. Many's the time." Her companion brayed with laughter and gave Daisy a broad wink. "It's me . . . Lottie Struthers from old Ranchipoor. This is me brother, Bert. 'Member Bert?"

Although the afternoon had turned cool, beads of sweat began to form on the Captain's upper lip. "I beg your pardon, madame. I have never seen you before," he said, grasping Daisy by the arm. "Now if you will excuse us . . ."

Lottie's eyes narrowed even more and the

feathers of her boa stood up stiffly in the wind. She looked like a small, enraged cat.

"Ho, so that's the way of it. Finally got your heiress, eh? Don't want to remember old Lottie what knew'd you 'fore you started after the debs. Just you watch it, missie," she said swinging around to confront Daisy. "It's your money he's after, mark my words."

Daisy lost her temper completely. How *dare* this insolent woman malign her handsome escort and threaten to ruin her day. She surveyed Lottie from head to toe and remarked in a voice like ice, "Captain Brothers is no fortune hunter. He is with me . . . and I have no money *at all.*"

"Come along, Lot," muttered her brother, dragging Lottie off. " 'Course Dickie don't want to recognize you. You're queerin' his pitch." He twirled the ends of his mustachios and calmly undressed Daisy with his eyes. "Can't say that I would mind havin' a go meself, what!" He brayed with laughter as he led his sister off along the deck.

Daisy found that she was still trembling with rage—so much so that she was unaware that Captain Brothers had put an arm around her waist. "Pay no attention," he was saying. "It's obviously a case of mistaken identity, or that pair are stark, raving mad. I say, Daisy, don't look like that. Don't let that terrible pair spoil our day."

Daisy gave him a weak smile and then blushed as she became aware of his arm around her waist, and moved a little away. The Greenwich Observatory was just coming into view and the passengers were collecting their belongings, preparing to disembark.

Captain Brothers reserved a table at the dining room window of an inn called The Cardinal which had tottered picturesquely at the edge of the water since Tudor times. The sun sparkled on the diamond panes of the bow windows and Daisy felt all her happiness returning.

Little sunny prisms of light danced in the wineglasses and across the silver. Captain Brothers was once again talking about India, the splendid sunshine, the bizarre sights and sounds of the markets, the majesty of the huge elephants, and the scares of the tiger hunt. Visions of peacocks and ivory, rubies and pearls—and in her mind's eye, two figures walked slowly in the moonlight in front of the Taj Mahal—danced in front of Daisy's dazzled eyes.

At last Captain Brothers edged his chair closer. "Y'know, Daisy, I think it was magnificent the way you stood up to that madwoman and lied about having no money." He gave his charming laugh. "That certainly put her in her place."

Daisy looked at him with some surprise. "But I haven't any money. I do have an allowance from my father. But I understand that I have no dowry. Poor Papa! I wonder how he can manage to send as much as he does."

Unaware that her partner had suddenly been turned to stone, she prattled on happily. "I've never met my father, you know. It was amazing how it all happened. You see I had been brought up as Daisy Jenkins, but the lady I believed to be my aunt was in fact an old servant of my father's and . . . and . . . Is anything the matter?"

Captain Brothers's charming laugh seemed a trifle forced. "No, of course not. Here! I say, you! Waiter!"

"Sir?"

"Bring the whole brandy decanter, will you? And jump to it, man."

Daisy recommenced her narrative, but once again her voice faltered off into silence. Captain Brothers seemed to be downing large goblets of brandy, one after the other.

Daisy tried again. "Oh, I would so like to see India. The way you described it. All sunshine and flowers . . ."

"And heat and flies and dust and damned natives and bloody mess bills," said her companion thickly, addressing his goblet. "And the Colonel's wife supervising all the gels like a damned governess." His voice suddenly rose to a high falsetto. "Don't go near that *dreadful* Captain Brothers, gels. No prospects, I *assure* you."

Daisy looked at him in bewilderment, her childish mouth beginning to tremble. "But all the lovely stories you told me . . . about . . . about the flowers and how pretty . . ."

"Oh, tommyrot!" he interrupted her rudely. "*That* was when I thought you had money."

Anger drove the tears of mortification from Daisy's eyes. She got to her feet and her voice rang around the small dining room. "You, sir. You are no gentleman!"

His eyelids, which had begun to droop, flew up and a cynical gleam flashed through the drunken sea of his blue eyes like a surfacing shark. He raised his glass. "That's the stuff, Daisy. Daughter of the regiment, and all that. Thump the tub, fly the flag, stiffen the upper lip. Captain Brothers is not a gentleman." The clouds of drunkenness closed in and he began to mutter, "What a waste of money. Hire of brougham, hire of coachman, pay the meal . . ."

Daisy half opened her reticule to throw money on the table and then closed it again with a snap.

"No! I shall *not* give you any money. I hope the expense of today hurts you in your pocket because I think that is the only way you *can* be hurt. Here! Here's a wreath to put on the graveyard of your hopes, sir!"

She swept a bouquet of roses out of their vase on the table and crammed them. thorns and all, on top of his head and then fled from the room.

Captain Brothers sat for a long time over his brandy, the water from the roses trickling slowly down his handsome face like tears.

"Captain Richard Brothers! Good God! The pair of you must be mad!"

His Grace, the Duke of Oxenden paced up and

down the Nottenstones' drawing room, the scarlet silk lining of his evening cloak flashing as he moved.

"But, my dear Toby," wailed the Countess. "Are you absolutely *sure*. He is *so* handsome."

The Duke took a deep breath. "Richard Brothers is a fortune hunter, a notorious cardsharp, and an unpleasant drunk. Harry Trenton told him that Daisy was an heiress. The silly chump meant it as a joke. Dammit! If Brothers still thinks Daisy has money, he'll be trying to seduce her. If he's found out she hasn't and he's been drinking, he may very well seduce her all the same, out of spite. He's got a filthy temper."

"But how can we find out where they've gone? They went off in a very smart carriage."

The Duke ceased his angry pacing. "Brothers hasn't got a carriage. He must have rented it. I'll send someone around to the livery stables and I'll wait here to see if there's any news."

Angela, Countess of Nottenstone, surveyed the Duke from under lowered lashes. "Dear me!" she said in a deceptively mild voice. "You haven't fallen for our little Daisy, have you, my dear Toby? *Such* anxiety!"

"Balderdash! Absolute twaddle, Angela. I have a natural concern that any young innocent girl should be in the paws of a cad like Brothers. And, may I add, my anger has been heightened by your very patent lack of concern."

Angela shrugged. "Don't *glower* in that antique

aristocratic manner at me," she said petulantly. "Maybe a seduction is just what she needs. All that damp and dewy innocence can be a teensy bit wearing."

The Duke threw up his hands and then resumed his pacing. The Earl and Countess watched him for a while and then began to giggle behind his back like naughty children with an irate parent. Then they started to make paper darts with messages like "Do you think he'll wear out the carpet?" and launched them to each other. Both were weeping with suppressed mirth by the time a footman arrived with the news that Captain Brothers and Miss Chatterton had taken a sail to Greenwich and Captain Brothers had sent the carriage back to the livery stables at the back of St. James's.

"I shall go and meet them at the pier," said the Duke stiffly. "Oh, don't be such a silly ass!" The last remark was to the Earl who was pantomiming a horsewhipping.

A glorious fiery sunset was flaming across the evening sky as the Duke of Oxenden waited for the arrival of the Greenwich boat. Down the river, the spars and masts of the ships at anchor stood out black against the burning sky like the charred remnants of a forest fire.

He began to feel foolish standing on the edge of the pier in his evening clothes. Perhaps she would not be on the next boat. Perhaps he was being overly concerned for her welfare. Perhaps she would misinterpret his concern.

Then he saw the steamer chugging toward the pier, lurching drunkenly on one side as the passengers gathered along the rail facing the shore.

He saw Daisy almost at once, standing in the bow, her arm raised to keep a ridiculous confection of pink tulle on her hair.

She waited, motionless, until almost all the passengers had left, and then she turned and made her way with little mincing steps down the gangplank.

The Duke moved forward to meet her, still hoping that Daisy would not think that he was in any way in love with her. But she merely regarded him silently with a mixture of tiredness and irritation. The Duke suddenly realized that Daisy regarded him as a sort of overwhelming parent who was forever finding her in the wrong.

She did not ask what he was doing waiting on the pier, but burst out with, "Well, how was I to know he was a masher?"

The Duke smiled and led her toward his carriage. "No way at all, my dear. Captain Brothers is reputed to have great charm when he is heiress hunting."

"I don't know *why* he should consider me an heiress," said Daisy crossly.

Perhaps, because of your impeccable taste in dress," drawled the Duke, eyeing the pink organza with an appreciative eye. He did not feel like betraying his friend Harry Trenton. "And on the subject of hunting, are you not tired of searching for the man of your dreams?"

Daisy was indeed tired. She felt very disillusioned, very young, and very silly. But she was not going to back down. A bet was a bet.

"I am not searching as you put it, Your Grace . . . I mean, Toby. I am like any other girl having her first Season. I am looking for a suitable young man."

"Then you are not like 'any girl,' " said the Duke. "Most would shudder to admit that that is their role in life. I notice that the new wave of women's emancipation does not seem to have touched you."

Dairy looked out at the jumbled lights of nighttime London. "Oh, I agree with the women's movement," she said with an odd maturity. "But I am no leader and no world changer. I could become a nurse or a stenographer and work hard for a pittance. I may yet have to become a governess. But strange as it may seem I would like love, a home, children."

She continued, almost talking to herself, "Perhaps I have been trying too hard. Perhaps I have been too trusting." She gave a little shiver and turned to the Duke. "I shall not go anywhere again unchaperoned without first finding out as much as I can about the gentleman."

"Really, Daisy," he mocked. "You are alone with me. I am glad I do not make you nervous."

"Oh, no," she said seriously, looking at him

wide-eyed in the light of the carriage lamps. "I feel quite comfortable with you . . . that is, when you don't make me feel like a guilty schoolgirl. You are like a sort of uncle."

Now the Duke of Oxenden was well aware of his attraction for the opposite sex. He had been courted and toadied to all his life. Women hung around the doorstep of his town house waiting for a glimpse of the "handsome Duke." Society women wrote him impassioned verses and even sent him flowers.

He found to his surprise that Daisy's remark about him being a sort of uncle annoyed him immensely. It was high time he gave Miss Daisy Chatterton less of his distinguished attention.

He pulled the high collar of his opera cloak around his ears and pretended to go to sleep.

"Don't sulk," said an infuriating voice from the opposite corner.

Impertinent child! He was not sure that he liked her at all!

Chapter Eight

The London Season had nearly come to an end. Daisy had done the rounds—Ascot, Henley, Goodwood, ball after ball and party after party. The novelty had worn off and she felt tired and somehow rootless. The Nottenstones' town house was charming with its huge bowls of flowers and frivolous cane furniture and bright wallpaper, but it managed to convey the very essence of impermanence. It was not a home to be lived in all year round and sometimes Daisy could not help wishing there were a few dogs or children around to break up the impeccable facade.

The grand marble staircase seemed to have been expressly designed for the Nottenstones to make stately descents or furious and dramatic exits. The conservatory appeared to have been built on so that indiscreet and intransient amours could take place behind the potted palms. The music room was for changing partners, and the library, an ideal place to make an assignation. The whole gave the impression of a stage set with the couples changing their affections with all the complexity and intrigue of a Restoration comedy.

In Upper Featherington one "walked out," became engaged, got married, and never looked at another man again—or that was the way Daisy remembered it. Seen from a distance, her old life seemed safer and more permanent. Society seemed to adore the artificial. Love of nature was damned as "too boring."

Driving in the park with the Earl one afternoon, Daisy had suddenly cried out, "What beautiful beeches!" "Never heard of 'em," remarked the Earl cheerfully. "New family in town, eh?"

She had tried to flirt with various young men, but her experiences with Freddie Bryce-Cuddestone and Captain Brothers had soured her in some way. She could not put her heart to it. The infuriating Duke of Oxenden had retired in the middle of the Season to his estates and she found herself missing his company.

Daisy was increasingly puzzled at her father's silence. Why not send her allowance to her direct? Why send it to Curzon? But Curzon was ready with the answer and Daisy did not know it had been long rehearsed. Curzon explained that he had been in Lord Chatterton's service as a footman a long time ago. Lord Chatterton was old-fashioned in his ways and would not let a woman handle money directly. He relied on his old servant to manage Daisy's financial affairs.

Slowly a plan began to form in Daisy's mind. She ceased to buy new clothes, preferring to make over and alter those she already had. Although she still sent part of her allowance to the vicar in the East End, she decided to save the rest. Perhaps one day she would journey to France to meet her mysterious father. There must be some reason why he did not return. Perhaps he was ill? No, Miss Chatterton, replied the ever-ready Curzon. His lordship was in excellent health.

Daisy began to study timetables of trains and the Channel ferries and to dig out her old French primers. She had mentioned her idea once to Curzon, but he had looked so horrified that she decided to make her plans in secret. The sympathetic Amy had promised to go with her.

Daisy had almost made up her mind to leave before the end of the Season. Then she met Sir James Ffoulkes.

The Earl and Countess had thrown a masquerade party and when Daisy had first seen the tall, masked figure of Sir James across the ballroom, her heart had missed a beat. She had been so sure he was the Duke. He had the same soft, husky voice and the same teasing, ironical manner. She had run straight across the ballroom and tugged at the wide, slashed sleeve of his Tudor costume crying, "Toby, where *have* you been?" and then without waiting for an answer had begun to pour out all her troubles and frustrations. She had blushed with dismay when he had finally told her he was *not* the Duke of Oxenden, but wished heartily that he were, since the Duke seemed to hold her affections.

Daisy had blushed again and disclaimed. The Duke was an old friend, nothing more. Sir James had looked relieved. But with his undoubted elegance, heavy-lidded, cynical eyes, and man-of-the-world air, he did seem very like Oxenden and Daisy had warmed to him.

Daisy and Sir James were soon a familiar couple on the London social scene. Not all Amy's diligent ferreting could unearth anything doubtful or unsavory about Daisy's new escort. Sir James had been married to an American heiress who had recently died in New York and had left him a wealthy widower. He was charming and the ladies adored him. The gentlemen did not seem overly fond of his company, but Daisy put it down to masculine jealousy. She judged him to be around thirty-five years old.

Daisy was young and feminine enough to enjoy the jealous looks she herself received when the suave Sir James continued to single her out at ball or party. Daisy began almost unconciously to adopt the flirtatious manners of the more daring young girls of her social set, since it seemed to amuse Sir James and he seemed to realize that she was only joking. Their conversations became more intimate in a secondhand kind of way as they freely discussed the liaisons and affairs of various society members. Daisy began to feel very dashing and "up-to-date." Up-to-date was the latest slang word, as if the top ten thousand were determined to shrug off the last remnants of Victorian fuddy-duddiness.

Sir James's heavy-lidded eyes began to take on a predatory gleam as he watched Daisy's slim figure dancing through the ballrooms.

Her apparent innocence combined with her slightly naughty conversation was intriguing. She certainly could not be as innocent as she seemed. Her father was a cardsharp and she was being chaperoned by the Nottenstones whose affairs were legendary. Daisy danced and laughed and flirted and Sir James waited and watched like some elegant bird of prey.

Daisy had learned to avoid being made the butt of practical jokes or, if she could not escape, to take it in good part. She felt a much more sophisticated and worldly girl these days than the one who had fled in tears from the Trentons. Accordingly, when Lady Trenton came to call with an invitation to a house party at the Trenton country home, Daisy gladly accepted. Sir James had been invited and Lady Mary's mother, the Countess of Lenderton, was to supervise the whole event. Nothing could be more respectable!

The guests were to be taken to Wester Cherton, the Trenton home in Sussex, by special train from Paddington.

Champagne, lobster patties, game pie, and other delicacies had been freely served to the party on board the train and when they finally puffed into the small station of Wester Cherton village, Daisy felt sleepy and overfed.

The rest of the guests, who seemed to have a bottomless capacity for champagne, piled into the waiting carriages, cheering and laughing. One young man leapt on the box of Daisy's carriage and enthusiastically blew on a hunting horn right in the coachman's ear. Daisy wondered fleetingly for the hundredth time how some well-trained servants managed to keep their tempers. Roaring with laughter and all in tearing high spirits, they clattered up the long weedy driveway of Wester Cherton Manor.

The manor was a long, low, redbrick Tudor building which had recently had its brickwork cleaned and repointed and in the process had shed a great deal of its antique charm. It now appeared distressingly modern and naked, rather like a series of laborers' cottages all crammed together. There was a strong odor of dogs and bad drainage. The dark hallway was cluttered with horse brasses, bits of harness, whips, and polo sticks, and a stuffed horse's head glared at them mournfully from over the cavernous fireplace.

Daisy was just trying to work out in her mind why a stuffed horse's head should be shocking and a stuffed deer's not, when her hostess descended the oaken staircase trailing a multitude of lace shawls. During her visit, Daisy was never able to discover if her hostess was wearing a complete gown. The Countess of Lenderton seemed to be dressed from head to foot in a multitude of scarves, feathers, beads, stoles, shawls, and brooches. She was a small, stout woman with heavy, strong features which seemed familiar to Daisy and it took her a few minutes to realize that the Countess looked exactly like the horse over the fireplace. Her hair had been dyed a rich brown and she whinnied rather than laughed.

"Drunk—the lot of you," she whinnied in welcome. "Get to your rooms and sleep it off. Your own rooms, mind. I'll have no shenanigans here."

She stared around at her guests. "Know you all anyway. Except her." She pointed at Daisy. "What's yer name?"

"Daisy Chatterton."

"Daisy. Common name. Chatterton, eh. Better lock up the silver." She threw back her head and whinnied to the rafters. "No need to bridle, girl. I'm a plainspoken woman. Call a spade a shovel, what! Well, go on. Get along the lot of you. Drinkies at six."

Daisy was shown to her room and thankfully left alone with Amy. It was a low-raftered bedroom which smelled of dry rot and damp. It seemed nearly filled by an enormous brass bed. Daisy felt the coverlet and noted gloomily that that was damp as well as everything else. Great trees pressed against the window. Amy lit the candles and sniffed, "We should really leave by the next train, if you ask me."

"I know," agreed Daisy. "It's all pretty horrible. And she's horrible . . . the Countess, I mean. Silly old horse. But Amy, I can't leave. Sir James is coming."

Amy started to unpack and gave her mistress an enigmatic look. "You're sweet on him, ain't you?"

Daisy blushed and nodded.

"I dunno," said Amy slowly. "I can't find nuffink bad about him but he gives me the shivers."

"You're romanticizing," said Daisy lightly. "He's always behaved like a gentleman and goodness knows, he's had enough opportunity not to."

"I wish you wouldn't talk like that, Dais'," said Amy slowly. "Sort of fast-like. Might give some gents the wrong idea about you."

Daisy laughed. "Oh, it's up-to-date to speak like that, Amy. Everyone does it. Now lay out my dinner gown and then let me have a nap, there's a dear."

"I see you've dropped the idea of going to France."

"Not quite." Daisy picked nervously at the coverlet. "I've only bought one frock after all and I've got plenty of money saved."

After Amy had left, she lay on top of the damp bed lazily dreaming of Sir James and watching the leaves shifting and turning outside the window.

Promptly at six o'clock Daisy hesitated outside the drawing room, smoothing down her gown and listening to the chatter of voices inside. For some reason she could not define, she had a slight feeling of panic, almost like stage fright, and a longing to escape, but a footman was already at her elbow and throwing open the double doors.

There was a slight silence as she entered. Heads turned and Sir James caught his breath. She was dressed in a deceptively simple sheath of scarlet silk, cut low over the bosom and with long tight sleeves ending at points at the wrists. The soft childish beauty of her features combined with the daring sophistication of the gown made her look as exotic as a Beardsley drawing.

Daisy moved about the room, chatting to the guests and feeling increasingly uncomfortable. Most of the ladies seemed to have sort of lopsided smiles on their faces as they looked at her and even the cheeriest of young men subjected her to a kind of brooding stare.

Neither Mary nor Harry nor their hostess had, as yet, appeared. Sir James rang the antique bell on a massive sideboard. A frail, elderly butler appeared to inform them that my lord and lady and the Countess had left on a visit to a neighboring household and that the Earl was still at Cowes and not likely to return.

A young man called Bertie Burke seemed to be the angriest. "I say!" he expostulated. "This is downright cultivating eccentricity. We all know the Trentons like a joke but to run away and leave a whole house party on the day of their arrival is carrying things too far.

"Well, don't just stand there. Fetch up some refreshment."

"I am afraid that will not be possible, sir."

"In heaven's name why not?"

"Her ladyship keeps the keys to the cellars and to the liquor cabinet with her at all times, sir."

There were loud cries of dismay. Most of the guests were feeling the aftereffects of their celebrating on the train journey and felt in the need of a bracer. Daisy began to giggle. They all seemed to be in a state of shock. Bertie, who seemed to have been silently elected spokesman, tried again.

"Look here. We'll all just need to pack up and return to London."

"I regret, sir," said the butler with a kind of mournful enjoyment, "that the last train for London has already left."

More groans greeted this news and the guests began to look around nervously.

The room was dark and lit by candles, gaslight having obviously been considered an unnecessary expense. The furniture had not been renewed since the days of the Regency and what must have been once light and elegant and the latest in fashion, now stood around shabbily on its chipped and spindly legs. With the exception of the heavy sideboard, it all looked too frail and tired to cope with a rumbustious party of Edwardian sophisticates. There were three young men including Bertie, as well as Sir James and an elderly Colonel Witherspoon who seemed determined to relive the days of his youth. The ladies included three young debutantes who all looked small and foxy and giggled, Kitty, and a dashing widow named Jo Phillips who was almost as enraged as Bertie over the lack of stimulants.

"Well, we've got the carriages," said Bertie at last. "Is there an inn near here?"

"There is a place called The Prince of Wales Feathers, sir. About five miles along the Lewes road."

"Hooray!" cried Bertie. "Let's all go and drink up all the champers in the pub."

Noisy cheers and cries of assent greeted his suggestion. Everyone seemed suddenly anxious to get away from the dim and oppressive atmosphere of the manor. There was a bustling about, a summoning of maids, a collecting of wraps, and they all congregated cheerfully in the hall. "Wait a bit." cried Mrs. Phillips. "Oxenden's due to arrive."

"Leave him a note," chorused several voices. Sir James had noticed the start Daisy had given and the quick turn of her head. He took hold of her arm possessively. "Let's take a carriage to ourselves and get away from these rowdy children."

Daisy drew back slightly. She was suddenly nervous at the prospect of being alone with him, but the others were all pairing off and it seemed an unspoken fact that she should go along with Sir James. As if judging her nervousness, he released her arm and began to speculate lightly on the eccentricity of the Countess, making her laugh, and guiding her gently to a waiting carriage.

They were about to move off when the carriage door was wrenched open and Bertie Burke hurtled in and plumped himself down beside Daisy. "Can't leave you to monopolize the prettiest girl in the party, James," he said cheerfully. "Let's liven things up right away. Ever heard me sing, Miss Chatterton? No? Well, here we go . . ." He began to sing "Good-bye, Dolly Grey" in a pleasant tenor. After a few minutes, Daisy joined in in a clear soprano and Sir James sat in his corner watching them and feeling immeasurably old.

By the time they rolled into the courtyard of the Prince of Wales Feathers, Daisy was helpless with laughter at Bertie's antics and Sir James was regretting that the days of dueling were over.

The rest of the party had arrived before them and had ordered "all the champagne in the house" and expressed the determination to drink it all. Bertie immediately challenged Daisy to a game of Colonel Puff-Puff, a remigental sport requiring the loser to drink a whole glass of champagne without pausing for breath. Daisy lost five times and then retired from the game, saying she was feeling dizzy.

One by one the locals drank up and left, leaving the inn to their noisy and impertinent betters. Jo Phillips began to bang out songs on an old upright in the corner and Bertie, after ripping a chintz curtain from one of the windows to use as a skirt, gave a rousing imitation of a Cockney lady doing "Knees Up Mother Brown." He finished to a hearty round of applause and the ladies of the party, including Daisy, now all feeling very tipsy, joined him in the dance, giggling with laughter and coyly flashing their ankles. Jo Phillips got as far as flashing her garters and the landlord's wife stepped in to protest that "she wasn't running no bawdy house."

"Keep your dreary middle-class morality out of this," snapped Sir James, "or I shall have the local magistrate remove your license."

Daisy looked at him, sobered for the minute. Then she tried to tell him how much she disapproved of his manner, but the waves of drunkenness had come back and all the words seemed to come out the wrong way.

One of the young men, the Honorable Clive Fraser, produced a hunting rifle and, after setting up a row of glasses along the bar, proceeded to challenge the rest of the men to a shooting match. Again the landlord's wife rushed forward to protest, and Jo Phillips aimed a soda siphon at her face, drowning the poor woman's complaints, and then jumped on top of the bar, offering her garters as first prize.

Colonel Witherspoon had drifted into some drunken dream where he was in Imperial Russia and after each glass of champagne, he smashed his glass into the fireplace and called for his horse. One of the foxy girls was being sick in a corner and the other two were trying to set fire to the curtains.

Daisy grabbed hold of her remaining wits and pleaded with Sir James to take her back to the manor. Sir James had already spied the landlord's son leaving by the door and knew that it was only a matter of time before the local police force descended upon the inn.

Daisy stumbled into the courtyard of the inn. Far, far above her, a tiny moon reeled and swam through the clouds Its reflection raced through a puddle in the courtyard and Daisy suddenly felt as if she was standing on her head.

"You need fresh air, my dear." Sir James's voice seemed to come from very far away. "Let's take a little walk down the road."

Daisy agreed thankfully. She felt if she got back inside the stuffy carriage, she would be sick. Soon the sounds of merriment and crashing glass faded from her ears. They plunged into the gloom of a tunnel formed by arched trees, Daisy trying to bring her eyes back into focus and Sir James restlessly searching for a convenient place to sit down. Suddenly they turned a bend in the road and came to the edge of the trees. The moonlight washed over the empty fields spread on either side and far, far away a train whistled, opening up mental vistas of immeasurable plains of loneliness.

Sir James guided Daisy gently from the road, across a field, and settled her at the foot of a large oak. Unaware that he was standing looking down at her, Daisy leaned back thankfully and stared up at the gently moving leaves of the tree.

He sank down beside her and put his arms around her and began to kiss her very, very gently. It was pleasant to be kissed and stroked and caressed, thought Daisy lazily. He moved slightly and she shivered as a cold breeze crept across her breasts. A little warning bell of returning sobriety sounded far back in her brain. She looked down.

He had unfastened the scarlet dress at the back and slid it down over her arms to bare her breasts. She gave a little moan of alarm and tried to sit up, but he forced her back and then she felt the rough stubble of his chin against her chest as he passionately bit and kissed her breasts. The more she tried to push him away, the more excited he became. Daisy pushed at him with all her strength and found she was helpless. His mouth was wide open and fastened over hers like a gag, while his exploring hands started to fumble under her skirt.

What did all the sophisticated wit and elegance matter now? This heavy weight, gasping and muttering obscenities and groping around on top of her, was about as sophisticated as a gorilla. As fright sobered Daisy completely, her reaction became just as primitive. She wrenched herself free and screamed at the top of her voice. She then scrambled to her feet and stumbled across the wet grass of the field. Then she tripped and fell and twisted around to look up wide-eyed at her pursuer. He stood looking down at her, his eyes gleaming wetly in the moonlight. A slow smile curled his long mouth and he spread his large hands and reached down to her. Daisy closed her eyes.

There was a sound of running feet, a tremendous thud. She slowly opened her eyes.

Sir James lay sprawled on his back in the long grass. The Duke of Oxenden stood looking down at her.

"Good evening, Miss Chatterton," said the light, hesitant voice. "Dear me, what an exciting life you lead. Would you please cover yourself up or I shall be tempted to take over where Sir James left off."

Daisy rose to her feet and pulled her gown back onto her shoulders. "Before we leave the scene of battle," the Duke went on, "we had better find out just how far Sir James did go."

Sick and shaken, Daisy clung to him for support. "I have . . . been . . . raped . . ." she gasped.

The Duke turned a stony face toward the recumbent Sir James. "Then you had better wait for me at the edge of the fields, my dear," he said, in a deceptively gentle voice. "For I am to thrash the life out of this cad."

He took a step forward toward Sir James and then halted. He turned to Daisy once again. "Now you will answer my questions no matter how embarrassing they may be. Just pretend I am the uncle you believe me to be. Did he . . . remove your drawers?"

Daisy let out a faint squeak. "No . . . Toby . . . but he . . ."

The Duke suddenly smiled and took her arm. "One cannot rape a bosom, even one as beautiful as yours, my dear. Come along. We will return to the manor. You will get the excellent Amy to get you a hot drink and you will forget all about this."

"Forget about it!" cried Daisy. "How can I face that man again. After what he tried to . . ."

"Now, now," said the Duke, with infuriating calm. "We are not living in one of your romances. With all the opiate and drink you young things consume, this little scene has become pretty much an everyday affair at a house party.

"Good heavens, girl, if you insist on pickling yourself in champagne and wearing a gown that could be the envy of every Parisian courtesan, what else do you expect? Sir James is not entirely to blame, you know."

"But I wanted to be up-to-date," wailed Daisy.

"Being up-to-date in this society of ours seems to mean that one little virgin eggs the other on to say bold things and wear tarty gowns.

"The young ladies of your party are now, for example, under arrest, and are crying for their mothers like lost lambs. The unquenchable Mrs. Phillips, on the other hand, will be charged with assaulting an officer of the law."

"What did she do?"

"Using her garters as slingshots she bombarded the constables with champagne corks and used language that would make a sailor blush. All of the party are fortunately rich enough to pay for the damage and will only be read a lecture by the magistrate."

They had now reached the Duke's carriage and Daisy sat silently in the darkness. At last she said in a small voice, "I must offer you my apologies, Toby. I did behave very badly."

"You don't owe me any apologies. But, as I told you before, I cannot always be on hand to rescue you. Do try for a little more common sense."

"Oh, you always make me feel young and foolish," said Daisy. "Have you never been in love? Have you never done anything silly?"

"No," he said bluntly. "I came into my inheritance at an early age and by the time I had learned to handle my responsibilities, I already felt old and cynical. I had enough opportunities to learn that passion alone does not mean love. Practically all the marriageable girls I meet would gladly marry me for my title."

"And you are looking for true love," said Daisy gently.

He roared with laughter. "You forget, my romantical duckling, that I don't believe it exists. I enjoy my life very well and, in time, I shall marry someone suitable." He leaned his head against the squabs and looked at her thoughtfully. "Sometimes, of course, when I was much younger, the moonlight and champagne would play tricks and I would fancy myself in love."

"Love!" said Daisy dismally. "Are all the men going to be like beasts, and maul and grab?"

"Not necessarily," he teased. "Unless of course when you are so head over heels in love that you will be delighted when a man . . . mauls and grabs."

"Never!" said Daisy with a shudder. "Sir James seemed so elegant and poised that I thought . . ."

"You thought that he would make love in a cool and sophisticated manner . . . like this . . ."

He gently took her chin in his long fingers and placed a fleeting kiss on her lips. Daisy felt strangely breathless and dizzy. The effects of the champagne seemed to be coming back.

"Oh, you are always laughing at me," said Daisy. "You like to control the situation. I would love to see you being controlled for a change." She suddenly grinned mischievously, "What if *I* should suddenly begin to make love to *you*?" She wound her arms around his neck and leaned against him with a mock sigh. He closed his arms around her and looked down at her with an unreadable expression in his eyes.

"I should have thought this evening would have taught you not to play with fire, Daisy Chatterton."

"Oh, pooh!" laughed Daisy. "I'm only playing with my old Uncle Toby."

His grip tightened and he bent his head. His lips came down hard on hers and Daisy closed her eyes. The world spun away in a mixture of champagne bubbles and moonlight. She felt as if every bone in her body were melting.

His breathing was slightly ragged as he abruptly put her away from him. "There you are," he said in a husky voice. "Don't ever play with old Uncle Toby."

Whatever she was to reply, he would never know, for the carriage had come to a halt in front of the manor. The Duke swung off his evening cloak and placed it around Daisy's shoulders as they stood together in the driveway. He bent and kissed her forehead and led her into the house.

Harry Trenton was lounging under the horse's head and got to his feet when they came in. "So you escaped the long arm of the law," he laughed. "I gather the rest have been released and are on the road home."

"What on earth were you playing at, Harry, running off like that and leaving your guests stranded?" demanded the Duke.

Harry gave an enormous shrug. "Oh, Mother forgot all about a dinner engagement until the last minute. She thought you'd all be able to amuse yourselves pretty well but she forgot to give the cellar keys to Beskins." Beskins was the butler. "She has the long-standing belief that Beskins is a drunk although the poor old boy never touches the stuff. And when she remembered that you lot were boozeless, she merely pointed out that you'd all guzzled too much champers on the train anyway. Seemed to amuse her—the idea of you all being sober, I mean. Never thought you'd leg it for the nearest hostelry and start breakin' the place up.

"Fancy a game of billiards before turning in, Toby?"

"All right, Harry. Run along to bed, Daisy. Get a good night's sleep."

Daisy paused at the foot of the staircase and looked back at the Duke. But he had turned away laughing, his arm around Harry Trenton's shoulders. Obviously their kisses had meant nothing to him at all.

Amy was waiting in the bedroom and exclaimed with horror over the wreck of Daisy's gown. Unlike the Duke, she did not take Daisy's adventure lightly. "We've got to leave, Dais'. You can't meet him tomorrow."

Daisy sighed. "Oh, the Duke says it happens all the time."

"I don't like this here kind of society," said Amy roundly. "It's bad for you, Dais'. Why, in Upper Featherington, he would have had to marry you."

"Well, thank God we aren't in Upper Featherington," said Daisy. "Maybe the Duke is right. Maybe love doesn't exist."

"Yes, it does," said Amy, jerking the pins from Daisy's hair. "But it's based on respect and trust and having a bit of fun together. You ask for too much, Dais'. It's all them novels you read."

Amy paused and looked at the childish face in the mirror. "Just have a bit of common sense.

Don't get yourself alone with any chap until you've got the ring on your finger." She slipped Daisy's nightdress over her head and then leaned forward to blow out the candles.

"Leave them, Amy," said Daisy. "I want to think for a bit."

After she had gone, Daisy sat in an armchair by the window, turning over the events of the evening in her mind. The episode of Sir James Ffoulkes had been a disaster. She heard the noises of the returning guests and then doors slamming along the corridor as they returned to their rooms.

She rose wearily and crossed to the window. The leaves blew back like a curtain exposing a moonlit square of garden. A couple stood clasped in each other's arms—the Duke and Mrs. Phillips. Then the leaves blew back over the window again.

Daisy had a sudden desire to cry.

In the garden below, the Duke of Oxenden deliberately unwound Mrs. Phillips's arms from his neck. "Go to bed, Jo," he said kindly. "You're squiffy."

"No man pushes me away l—like that," hiccupped Jo Phillips. "I'll make you pay." She stumbled into the hall and nearly collided with Sir James Ffoulkes. "Want to get even with Oxenden?" he said. "I have a little plan that may interest you. Come to bed and I'll tell you all about it. . . ."

Chapter Nine

Daisy struggled in the throes of a nightmare. She was strapped to a table and Mrs. Phillips was pouring champagne over her. No matter how she twisted and turned, the liquid kept pouring down on her face in a steady stream.

She awoke with a start and thought for one horrible minute that her dream had come to life. A steady stream of water was trickling down through the ceiling. She jumped out of bed and stood shivering on the rug. Trickles of water ran through the leaves outside and down the tiny mullioned panes of the window. Water descended on the roof with a steady roar.

Daisy tugged at the bell rope which came away in her hand. Amy came bustling into the room followed by a diminutive maid bearing cans of hot water.

"Get some footmen here to move the bed," ordered Amy after a quick look around. "Look Daisy. I actually found some dry wood. We'll have a fire going in no time. Lor' you should see the place. Water dripping everywhere. Evidently my lady spent a mint recently getting the outside cleaned and forgot to tell them to fix the roof. I heard her this morning saying to Lord Harry, 'Really, the way you all go on about a little water. When you come into your inheritance, dear boy, you can patch it up. I have spent enough.' And then she gives that horse laugh of hers."

She helped Daisy into a warm, blue-velvet dress and jacket and stood back looking pleased with the effect. "Now, you look more like your old self and less like a floozy."

"Really, Amy . . ."

"It's true. You looked a real tart in that red thing though I didn't like to say so at the time. Fact is Daisy, you need a mum . . . or a good strong husband."

"At the rate I'm going, it certainly looks as if I'm not going to find a suitable man. Let's go to France, Amy."

"Ask the Duke about it," was all Amy would say.

Daisy went down to look for the Duke of Oxenden. He at least could supply her with her father's address. She paused on the center of the oaken staircase and looked down into the gloomy hall. Footmen were placing more buckets under the leaks and carrying away ones that were already full. Bertie Burke clattered down behind her, seemingly none the worse for last night's roistering and carrying a large, black-silk umbrella over his head. "Like to share my brolly, Daisy?" he said cheerfully. "Honestly, new leaks keep springing up the whole time. That's a very fetching outfit."

Daisy smiled and thanked him. He had a pleasant round face with a slightly receding chin and small weak eyes which blinked at the world with unshakable good humor. "Perhaps I'll join you later," said Daisy. "At the moment I'm looking for the Duke."

"Good luck to you," said Bertie amiably. "I keep out of Oxenden's road myself. The day's chilly enough without having to endure that cold yellow stare. Wouldn't mind his money though. 'Cept I wouldn't like to work as hard as he does. He's keen on agriculture and all sorts of worthy stuff like that. Harry Trenton swears that he even works in the fields come harvest time. Now that's carrying democracy too far.

"Anyway, I'll see you later. Going to make some cocktails tonight if our horsey hostess can part with the keys. What's a cocktail? It's a superduper American invention. Super drinkies. Lift the top right off your pretty head. Toodle-oo."

He ambled off in the direction of the billiard room, waving his umbrella and dodging the drips.

Sir James and Jo Phillips were sitting together at the breakfast table. As Daisy entered the room Mrs. Phillips said something to Sir James and both burst out laughing. Daisy was surprised. She had thought Sir James would be too ashamed of his behavior of the previous night to put in an appearance. A slow blush crept up her face and she was the most embarrassed of the three.

She retreated quickly from the breakfast room and collided with the Duke of Oxenden who had just come down the stairs.

"Oh, Toby, may I have a word with you in private?"

"Certainly. I gather from the look on your face that you have just met James Ffoulkes." Daisy nodded mutely.

"And I also gather," he said leading her into the library and neatly sidestepping several buckets and ewers, "that he seemed quite unconcerned about the whole affair?" Again Daisy nodded. "Feel assured he has been in similar circumstances before," said the Duke. "Now, what is it that you want to see me about?"

Daisy sat down on a hard chair by the window. The upholstered ones looked too damp. "Please . . . could you give me my father's address in France? I think perhaps I might be able to travel soon to see him. I have the money from the sale of The Pines—Miss Jenkins's house—and also a small amount I have managed to save from my allowance."

The Duke sat down at a desk and started scribbling on a blotter with his back to her. What on earth could he say! He realized he had scribbled "ffinish Ffoulkes" over and over again and hurriedly scored it out.

He turned around slowly. "I feel that perhaps your father should invite you first, Daisy. And he did say that he would shortly be returning to England. I would need to write to my secretary. I do not have your father's address with me. You really cannot go traveling through France by yourself, you know."

"Amy has promised to go with me."

"Amy would not really be enough. You need a man to go with you. Perhaps that true love you're always talking about will come along."

Daisy's face closed up and the Duke cursed himself for the careless remark.

"Perhaps," said Daisy getting to her feet. She felt angry with him and disappointed. She felt obscurely that he should have offered to accompany her to France.

"Have you had breakfast?" asked the Duke abruptly.

"I didn't feel like any," said Daisy. "The sight of James and Jo Phillips with their heads together quite put me off."

"Probably plotting your downfall. . . . Oh, don't look so surprised. But be on your guard. They will probably just try to play some embarrassing practical joke. Come, now. I hear the others coming downstairs. We shall go together and eat something . . . provided, that is, that the breakfast room is not under water."

Daisy was still smarting from his remark about "true love." But the thought of facing the others on her own was too daunting. The struggle was evident on her face and she saw the Duke regarding her with some amusement.

"Oh, my lord Duke!" cried Daisy, stamping her foot. "How I would love to see you making a fool of yourself . . . just once."

"Should that ever happen," he said lightly, "I will send for you posthaste."

The atmosphere in the breakfast room was electric. The Countess was in full voice, berating the guests for their "libertine" behavior in The Prince of Wales Feathers. The young members of the party were glaring at her sulkily, feeling trapped. The deluge had washed away part of the railway line and no one knew when it would be repaired. Escape seemed impossible.

If I were on a desert island, these are not the people I would choose to be marooned with, thought Daisy.

The faces, united and anonymous in the hectic drinking of the night before, had resolved into separate faces and identities.

There was a young woman in her early twenties called Ann Gore-Brookes who tittered a lot. She was the only person Daisy had ever known who actually said "tee-hee" when she laughed. She had a long indeterminate nose, eyes set close together, and an abundance of improbable red hair. She had attached herself to the Honorable Clive Fraser, a young man with luxuriant mustaches, a natty line in waistcoats, and large, wet eyes. A young debutante of Daisy's age who also had a long nose and close eyes but a head of sandy hair, so sparse that the pads showed through, turned out to be Lady Cynthia Wampers. She was accompanied by her brother, Lord Albert, who wore a large paint-brush mustache, a lot of oil on his hair, and who was marked by a lugubrious air of hangover and general defeat. Apart from the Trenton family, the Duke, Sir James, Jo Phillips and Bertie Burke, the remaining member of the party was a Miss Thomasina Forbes-Bennet, who had the same fox-like appearance as her two friends, Lady Cynthia and Ann Gore-Brookes, with ginger hair, a long nose, and closely set eyes. Colonel Witherspoon had left for his own home which was close by.

At that moment every shawl draped around the Countess seemed to be bristling with fury, and the more she berated her young guests, the sulkier they became until her son, Lord Harry Trenton, cut through her complaints with "Look, mother. Put the stopper on it right now. It was all our fault for beetling off and leaving them to their own devices on the first night. So give your tongue a rest."

Everyone looked at the formidable Countess in surprise, expecting another outburst, but she suddenly smiled weakly, picked up the morning paper, and barricaded herself behind it.

The rain continued to pour down outside in a

steady stream. A footman came in followed by a small boy carrying a basket of logs and soon there was a fine blaze crackling up the chimney.

Huge puddles were forming outside on the lawns and the ancient Sussex trees that always looked wet anyway, their trunks being coated in damp green slime, gleamed with sheets of rainwater as though frozen in ice. Black and purple clouds tumbled over the sky driven by some wind, high and faraway above the motionless bushes and trees of the estate.

Beyond the estate an infinity of waterlogged patchwork fields and gray and brown hills rolled down to meet the sea.

The Countess's unexpected silence combined with the crackling warmth of the fire revived the flagging spirits of the guests. "What you all need is a bracer," said Lord Harry, ordering a couple of magnums of *Veuve Cliquot* from the cellar, and staring repressively at his mother who showed alarming signs of bursting forth again. Everyone began to plan an entertainment for the afternoon. Bertie Burke suggested they make up a band. Mrs. Phillips would play the piano and he would perform on the paper and comb. Ann Gore-Brookes said that she would—"tee-hee"—play the cymbals with two saucepan lids, Lord Albert Wampers volunteered in a deep, sad voice of mourning to play the spoons. Everyone looked at him in surprise, whereupon he blushed and said he was "damned good at it, don't you know" and hid his face in his champagne tankard. The Honorable Clive, amid much cheering, said he would play the wineglasses and proceeded to demonstrate how he could play a scale by altering the water levels in a row of crystal glasses. And the Honorable Daisy Chatterton said, "Perhaps Mrs. Phillips will play a tune on her garters."

For one long minute there was absolute silence, while everyone looked at Daisy as if they could not believe their ears and Daisy stared back at them and wondered desperately if she had actually said what she thought she had just said.

Then everyone burst out talking.

"Spiteful little cat." (Jo Phillips)

"I *heard* Daisy's a methodist, tee-hee." (Ann Gore-Brookes)

"The wildest women always put up a prim front." (Sir James)

"I *hate* these shy little girls with the die-away airs. They say the nastiest things in the sweetest little voices." (Lady Cynthia)

'I want to talk about my band. We'll call it Burke's Beauties or Bertie's Beaux . . ." (Bertie Burke)

"Or Bertie's Buglers." (Lady Mary)

"Or Battling Bertie's Bungling Banjo Band." (The Duke)

"I am really so very sorry, Mrs. Phillips," said Daisy in a small voice. "I meant to be funny and it just came out sounding horrible."

Unexpectedly the Countess put down her paper

and sailed in to Daisy's defense. "I know just what you mean, my dear," she roared. "Happens to me the whole time. Esther Huntingdon was showing off this great spavined mare at the last hunt. I kept thinking 'How awful. How could she buy such a nag' and 'fore I knew it I'd opened my mouth and said, 'What a simply awful-looking beast. Did you buy her to help out a friend in Queer Street?' Well, she ain't spoken to me since. Not, of course, that that's any great loss."

"Apology accepted," drawled Mrs. Phillips with a smile that did not reach her eyes. Daisy caught Sir James staring at her. His whole face was alight with malice. "Why, he hates me!" she thought with surprise.

It had been the presence and manner of Sir James and the others which had sparked off Daisy's rude remark. That these people could behave like guttersnipes in the local inn, get arrested by the police, that Sir James should try to rape her and then all of them sit around the breakfast table planning childish games as if nothing had happened . . . it was just too much.

She became aware that the house party was on the move. Lord Harry had said there was an old music room on the first floor and he believed there was a box of tambourines and things like that in one of the cupboards. Bertie held out his arm to Daisy, his myopic eyes shining with good humor. "Come along, Daisy, you can sing for my band."

She held back, looking over her shoulder at the Duke, but he smiled and shook his head. "I have letters to write, Miss Chatterton, but I shall see you this evening and sit at your feet and admire your beauty." His voice was mocking, but his eyes held a warmth that Daisy had not noticed before. Daisy felt less alone and oddly comfortable. She accepted Bertie's arm and moved off with him.

Sir James followed with Jo Phillips. "Did you notice that *very* interesting exchange of glances, my dear? Perhaps we could kill two birds with one stone. . . ."

Chapter Ten

The music room, which was on the first floor of the east wing, was thankfully dry, being protected by the bedrooms above.

The rooms downstairs adjoining the front part of the great hall jutted out from the main part of the building and seemed to receive the full force of the deluge.

Daisy looked around her with pleasure. Fires burned at either end of the long low-ceilinged room, their flames reflected in the highly polished boards of an ancient oak floor. There was a spinet, a harpsichord, and a harp against one wall and a small audience of rout chairs lined up by the windows as if awaiting more courtly company of a bygone age. There was a pleasant scent of beeswax, applewood, and wine. Tall candles burned steadily from gold sconces on the walls, banishing the gloom of the dreary day.

"I say. This is more the thing, eh what!" said Bertie. "After all that pesky damp and gloom downstairs, I feel as I've been washed ashore on a warm island. Now, what about Bertie Burke's Blinking Brilliant Boggling Band?"

"I wonder if this thing still plays," Jo Phillips said, sitting down at the spinet. She was wearing an unrelieved black gown with a high-boned collar. It accentuated her creamy skin, large black eyes, and glossy black hair. Her long, thin fingers flicked over the keys and her elegant back was as straight as a ramrod.

A fine seat on a spinet, thought Daisy illogically, wondering why she disliked the woman so much.

The spinet sent out a tinkling, catchy tune and Mrs. Phillips began to sing,

"Sweet Molly O'Morgan
With her little organ
She's out on the streets every day
She's out on the streets every day
Singing tooral-a-rooral-a-rooral-i-ay . . ."

"Oh I s—say," stammered Bertie. "Ladies present and all that I mean, Jo, well after all. It's a bit warm, what?"

"Come, come, Bertie," laughed Mrs. Phillips. "Such a sweet, simple, little song. *You* don't find it offensive do you, Daisy?"

Daisy shrugged by way of reply and turned to look out of the window. She certainly could find nothing up with the song, but from the winks and grins of the other members of the party, she was well aware that it must be less innocent than it seemed.

"*I* know," said Ann Gore-Brookes. "We'll sing 'Daisy.' "

"What a good idea," said Sir James. "You must get down on one knee, Bertie, and sing it to our own Daisy."

Daisy wished that there was a medicine she could take to stop herself from blushing. She could feel the telltale red of embarrassment climbing up her cheeks as they all joined in the chorus:

"Daisy Daisy
Give me your answer do.
I'm half crazy
All for the love of you. . . ."

After the song was finished, Daisy cried, "What about your band, Bertie?" and successfully distracted the guests' attention from herself. They all bustled about finding various instruments and the Honorable Clive rushed off downstairs to collect his wineglasses after failing to rouse any servants.

He came back after a few minutes carrying a trayful of rattling glasses and bursting over with news. "You'll never guess what old boots and saddles has been and gone and done." Daisy gathered that old boots and saddles was a nickname for the Countess. "She's gone and given the whole staff the afternoon and evening off. 'Why?'

I asks. 'Oh,' says she, 'It's the anniversary of my dear mother's death. I *always* give *all* the servants some time off.' Don't want to be rude, Harry, but don't you think your mater carries things too far?"

"Course, she does. But it's her house and she can do as she likes. Only thing to do is get the cellar key from her before she retires for the day."

"Got it!" said Clive triumphantly. "Told me to give it to Sir James for safekeeping. Says he's the oldest since she can't find Oxenden."

"But what do we do about lunchies?" wailed Thomasina Forbes-Bennet.

Clive looked momentarily nonplussed. Then he brightened. "We can raid the kitchens and get some provender for ourselves. Fun, what."

"Absolutely ripping," drawled Jo Phillips. "But who, my darlings, is going to empty all those buckets of rainwater? I am not, for one. After all, servants are servants. Do one teensy thing for them and they get all sorts of sickening radical ideas into their little noodles."

Everyone murmured in agreement except Daisy and Bertie. "We'll jolly well just paddle," said Lady Cynthia in a militant kind of way.

The band organized itself and whumped out a few loud and unmusical tunes until the idea of raiding the kitchen seemed to be more attractive. They descended in a jolly, cheering mob, ate far too much, and left a considerable amount of debris behind. Silence fell on the old mansion as the guests retired to their rooms for an afternoon nap.

Sir James neatly divested himself of his clothes and arranged them on a chair in Jo Phillips's bedroom. "We're about to make love, not have a prizefight," she teased him. "Why are you looking so grim?"

"I'm plotting," he said thoughtfully, standing naked except for his black socks and suspenders, in the center of the room, and looking at the key in his hand. He tossed it lightly up and down and then said, "I feel sure I could put this cellar key to good use. What do you think about luring Oxenden and Daisy Chatterton down to the cellars and locking them in for the night?"

"Ridiculous," answered his companion sourly. "They'll roar their heads off."

"Can't hear a thing from down there once the door is closed," replied Sir James succinctly. "And the revenge is this: Oxenden will have to marry her if they spend the night down there together."

"Rubbish," yawned Jo, beginning to feel bored. "The old Countess will simply swear blindly they were chaperoned."

"No, that she won't," he grinned. "Dear, old-fashioned Victorian, is our hostess. She'll have Oxenden at the altar with a shotgun in his back if necessary. And Oxenden will be furious. He may have a gleam in his eye for Miss Chatterton, but he don't mean marriage. The proud Duke won't want his precious name to be tied to that of Chatterton."

He suddenly grinned. "What do you think they'll do down there all night?"

Jo Phillips stepped out of her stays and moved languidly toward the bed. "What will they do?" she mocked. "Why, come here, my dear Sir James, and let me show you. . . ."

The party had elected to meet at six in the evening in the music room. The rain still poured down with unremitting violence and Bertie, who had descended to the cellars to get the ingredients for his cocktails, reported cheerfully that all the buckets and pails and ewers under the leaks were nearly full to overflowing.

"Your mother's going to lose her good wines if that stream at the back of the house overflows," said the Duke of Oxenden to Harry Trenton. "Don't you think we should get organized and rescue them?"

Harry shrugged his great shoulders until he nearly burst the seams of his evening jacket. "I don't feel like doing anything about it. It's mother's concern. I've told her time and again that she runs a sloppy household and she just tells me to mind my own business. So I'm minding it."

"But don't you think it a trifle eccentric," pursued the Duke, "to get us all down here and find there are no servants, no dinner, as far as I can see, and no means of escape?"

"I forgot about grannie's anniversary," said Harry. "Honestly. Anyway, it adds a bit of adventure to have to rough it for a bit."

"This," declared Bertie, holding aloft something that looked like a silver bomb, "is a cocktail shaker."

"And what do you put in that lethal machine?" asked Ann Gore-Brookes.

For a moment Bertie looked nonplussed. It had sounded intriguing when the American friend had explained it, but for the life of him he could not remember what was supposed to go into it. He suddenly brightened and said vaguely, "Oh, a bit of this and a bit of that" and proceeded to throw the contents of several bottles haphazardly into the cannister. "Now I need ice," he declared.

"Ice!" exclaimed Lady Mary. "You mean chilled, surely."

"No. Ice. Definitely ice."

"Well, we haven't got any so you'll just have to hang that thing outside the window."

"We'll pretend it's *iced,*" said Bertie hopefully. He shook the cocktail shaker so energetically that his lank hair fell over his forehead in damp streaks. Then he poured a pale-green liquid into the glasses and started to pass them around. The Duke took a sip, muttered something about *Crème de Menthe* and sherry, and put his drink down. The rest drank theirs, declaring it to be everything from super to interesting to downright foul. But everyone decided it certainly had an energizing effect and called for more. While Bertie was busy again with the shaker, Daisy glanced across at Sir James Ffoulkes. There was almost an expression of waiting for something on his face. Daisy wondered what it could be. Sir James was, in fact, waiting for them all to become slightly drunk before putting his plan into action.

When the voices had reached a noisy crescendo, Sir James jumped up on a chair. "Silence, everybody," he cried. "I suggest we play Hunt the Guests."

"Whassat?" giggled Lady Cynthia and then cleared her throat and enunciated very clearly and distinctly. "I mean to say . . . what kind of game is that?"

"Well, it goes like this," said Sir James. "We all draw straws and the two guests that have the shortest straws are taken away and hidden—by me. Then the rest of you have to find them."

Heard through a rosy haze of Bertie's cocktails, it seemed a first-rate game. Sir James mysteriously had the straws already. Daisy and the Duke drew the shortest straws.

"Have summore drinkies before you go," beamed Bertie.

The Duke opened his mouth to say that no, he did not want to play such a childish game, but then he looked across at Daisy. She seemed happy and relaxed and very, very young and vulnerable, in a gown of light-green tulle, the color of spring leaves. He shrugged and smiled and allowed Sir James to lead them off along an infinity of low and narrow passages and steep back stairs until they reached the cellars.

"We won't be here long before we're found," remarked the Duke. "Bertie will be along soon to look for more cocktail mixtures."

"Oh, well. It's just a game," said Sir James lightly. "In you go."

The Duke held a candle in its pewter holder high above his head and took Daisy's arm to lead her down the steps. "We may as well see what wines our good hostess has," he said, and then stopped abruptly on the stairs as he heard the heavy door slam behind them and the sound of the key being turned in the lock.

"Now what's Ffoulkes up to?" he exclaimed. "I'm sorry, Daisy. I have a feeling that this may be his idea of revenge. He somehow hopes to keep us down here all night together, the idea being that I will have to marry you."

"But the other guests will tell everyone it was just a game," said Daisy. His face looked so stern, she tried to comfort him. "Don't worry. I won't marry you."

He gave a bitter laugh. "You may have to, my dear, if the Countess hears about this. She'll raise such an alarm and hue and cry that I will have no peace until I lead you to the altar." He sat down heavily on a wine cask. "What a mess!"

Daisy felt irrationally piqued. "There are worse things, my lord Duke, than being married to me."

That made him laugh and he raised the candle to look at her. She stood glaring indignantly at him like an angry kitten. "We'll worry about it all if and when it happens," he said. "Come, and I'll take you on a tour of the cellars. These are supposed to be the remains of a Roman villa."

Huge banks of wine racks soared up into the blackness: Burgundies and clarets, Rhine wines, Madeira, port, and champagne. The Duke began an amusing lecture on the merits of each vintage and Daisy heard not a word. She was attractive enough to have gained a certain feeling of power over the opposite sex during her Season. But she was never, at any time, very sure of herself and the fact that the handsome Duke would not welcome marriage to her made her feel very young, unsophisticated, and uninteresting. Her mind shied away from the fact that he may not have considered the idea of marriage to her because of their relative social positions. Daisy had been long enough in the social world to realize that an English Duke was a very grand personage indeed.

She suddenly became aware that her aristocratic companion was swearing fluently and not, it appeared, over a bad year. The Duke was holding the candle high above his head and Daisy heard, for the first time, the steady sound of rushing water. From a small barred window, high up on one of the walls, water was pouring down into the cellar, glistening in the candlelight like oil.

"Let's get back to the stairs," snapped the Duke, "and let's pray that that fool Ffoulkes means to let us out soon."

Upstairs, the guests and Lord Harry and Lady Mary had reassembled in the music room after searching without success for the missing couple.

All had downed several large measures of Bertie's transatlantic concoctions and were feeling the effects. Ann Gore-Brookes had "tee-heed" helplessly all over the house and had finally relapsed into maudlin and drunken tears. With what was left sober in his brain, Bertie registered with some surprise that she actually said "boo-hoo" when she cried.

The Trentons had their heads together plotting an ingenious booby trap. Lady Cynthia Wampers and Miss Thomasina Forbes-Bennet had discovered that they hated each other. The one would make some devastatingly bitchy remark to the other and then they would both sit back panting, resting on their metaphorical lances before the next joust. Lord Albert Wampers was refereeing the tournament in a sleepy way, interrupting the worst remarks with a "Ah, harrumph, I say, what. Steady on! Steady on!" The Honorable Clive Fraser was asleep. Jo Phillips was moodily tinkling on the spinet, and Sir James Ffoulkes calmly surveyed the room with only a slight drooping of the lids to indicate that he was not as sober as he appeared.

Bertie began to feel obscurely that there was something badly wrong. His wits were never too nimble, but they had been momentarily sharpened with alcohol and a growing concern for that deuced pretty girl, Daisy Chatterton. He saw James Ffoulkes and Mrs. Phillips exchanging enigmatic looks and he didn't like it. And, being Bertie, decided to say so.

"I say," he said loudly. "I don't like it."

"Well, you made the beastly drinks," remarked Sir James languidly.

"I'm not talking about the drinks. I'm talking about Miss Chatterton."

"Don't like Miss Chatterton?" said Sir James deliberately obtuse. "Now why, I wonder."

"Oh, don't be a silly ass," said Bertie, pushing his lank hair out of his eyes. "Hadn't we better let Oxenden and Miss Chatterton know that we can't find 'em and they can come out now?"

Harry Trenton looked up. "Hey, Bertie's got a point there."

"This is rather embarrassing," said Sir James smoothly. "I did endeavor to bring Toby and Daisy back to the party, but they . . . er . . . led me to believe that they did not wish to be disturbed."

Bertie felt himself blushing with embarrassment. He should have thought of that, but again there was that mysterious interchange of glances between Sir James and Mrs. Phillips.

"The cellar," he suddenly cried. "I forgot about the cellar. I say. I bet that's where they are. I'll just nip downstairs and—"

Sir James stepped forward and put a restraining arm round Bertie's thin shoulders. "Don't you know when you're not wanted Bertie, old chap? Mix us up some more of that splendid potion, there's a good boy. . . ."

"What a way to end," said the Duke of Oxenden. He and Daisy were standing on the cellar steps watching the black water slowly rising in the light of their guttering candle. "The stream in the grounds must have burst its banks."

The couple had tried beating on the door and shouting, but the ancient door was too thick for any sound to carry through it.

The candle gave one final brave spurt of flame and went out, leaving them in a damp, dark blackness.

The Duke put an arm around Daisy's slim body and held her close. She was shivering uncontrollably. She felt his long fingers pass lightly over her face. "Crying Daisy? Come now. I suggest we wait until the last minute and then swim across to the tallest of the wine racks and climb up as far as we can. Then the water should start flooding under the door and someone is bound to notice."

"I can—can't swim," stammered Daisy through chattering teeth.

"I can," said the Duke, "and provided you do exactly what I tell you to, I can get you over there with me." There was a rustling sound beside her.

"You're not taking off all your clothes," squeaked Daisy.

"No, my beloved goose, I am merely removing this hellish hard collar and boiled shirt, my jacket and shoes. I suggest you remove those heavy stays."

A strangled, shocked noise reached his ears.

"Now, now, Daisy," he said gently. "I can't see a thing in this pit. Take off your stays and put your dress back on."

With a touching little sob she began to fiddle with the fastenings of her dress, and the Duke of Oxenden realized with some surprise that this tantalizing striptease in the dark was uncomfortably erotic. He was relieved when he heard the crash of the heavy whalebone stays being dropped on the steps, a quick rustling, and a small voice saying, "I'm ready now."

"Now stand behind me and put your arms tightly 'round my neck," said the Duke. "That's the girl. Now relax and go limp. Don't try to struggle or to swim yourself. Here we go . . ."

Bertie Burke peered into the cocktail shaker. "All gone," he said mournfully.

"Thomasina drank it *all*," said Lady Cynthia waspishly.

Thomasina rounded on her, bristling with anger. With their ginger hair, long noses, and narrow closely set eyes, they looked like two battling foxes.

"Didn't," snapped Thomasina. "Anyway, drink's the problem in *your* family . . ."

"Isn't!"

"Is!"

"Your mother drinks *gin.*"

"Your mother's got the *gout.*"

"Cat!"

"Tart!"

"Steady on! Steady the buffs!" said Lord Albert.

"I'll nip down to the cellar and get more supplies. Key, please, James," said Bertie.

"Oh, I think we have all had enough to drink," said Sir James. He took the cellar key out of his pocket and waved it to-and-fro. Bertie made a lunge for it and with one quick movement, Sir James dropped it into Jo Phillips's cleavage. "Now it's gone where you can't get it, young man."

Now Bertie was very, very worried. He became more than ever convinced that something was badly wrong. A picture of Daisy's innocent, childish face swam suddenly before his eyes and in a flash, he realized that the Honorable Miss Daisy Chatterton would not do anything to offend the proprieties. Summoning up the ghosts of his crusading ancestors, Bertie suddenly electrified the company by plunging his hand into Jo Phillips's bosom, retrieving the key, and scuttling from the room before anyone could stop him.

"Let him go," he heard Sir James snarl. "The game's up."

Daisy Chatterton and His Grace, the Most Noble Duke of Oxenden, sat perched on the top of a wine rack, huddled together. The Duke had his arms wrapped tightly around her and her small head was tucked under his chin. After their plunge through the icy water and finding herself safe for the moment at least, Daisy had given up worrying. Toby seemed so large and capable and unconcerned. *How nice it would be,* she thought dreamily, *if somehow they* did *have to get married. How nice it would be to have a home, secure from the world, protected by someone who seemed to cope with life's battles so well.* She smiled in the darkness as she realized she had been dreaming of love in a cottage. Marriage to the Duke would mean life in a stately home and the awesome business of controlling a whole army of servants.

For his part, the Duke was prey to a series of novel and disturbing emotions. Passion he had felt on many occasions. But never this overwhelming feeling of tenderness. Dammit, he *would* kiss her. He searched in the darkness for her chin and turned her face up to his.

There was a frantic scrabbling at the lock, the cellar door flew open, and Bertie Burke stood there, the light from an oil lamp held above his head, streaming down the steps and shining on the black water.

Before they could cry out he had shouted "Daisy" and plunged into the water, oil lamp and all.

There were frantic gurglings and threshings and then his desperate cry of "I can't swim!"

"Silly chump," remarked the Duke ungratefully, plunging into the water. Bertie was dragged back to the steps by a firm hand and sent to get another lamp.

"Don't rouse anyone," said the Duke. "Miss Chatterton had to take off some of her clothes in order to swim. Just bring some lights, there's a good boy."

Bertie, who had been feeling like Sir Galahad a minute ago, thought that if anyone called him a "good boy" again, he would scream.

Daisy was helped down from her perch on the wine rack. Once again, she clasped her arms around the Duke's neck and entered the icy water. He swam powerfully to the cellar steps with a few strokes and helped her out.

They stood very close together, each one of them waiting for something and not knowing quite what it was. Bertie appeared, followed closely by Amy who was carrying a lamp in one hand and a blanket in the other.

Bertie's normally weak face seemed to have grown stronger lines. "You have had a very terrible experience, Miss Chatterton," he said. "Please allow me to escort you to London tomorrow. Dreadful people, you know. Not talkin' about you, Oxenden, but the rest of them . . . pah! Give me the goose bumps."

Daisy half turned and looked slowly at the Duke. She was waiting for him to offer his escort, waiting for him to make some little move to indicate that he cared for her in some way.

"Dammit," said the Duke. "I can't find my studs. I must have dropped them on the steps."

Daisy gave a tired little sigh and then smiled at Bertie. "I shall gladly accept your escort tomorrow, Mr. Burke. Come, Amy."

Bertie looked after her and then turned to stare triumphantly at the Duke.

But Oxenden was still searching for his studs.

Chapter Eleven

No one could deny that Bertie Burke had behaved splendidly. The morning after the cellar episode, he had ridden twelve miles in the still pouring rain to commandeer a motorcar from "some scribe chappie" in the distant neighborhood. The writer had cheerfully given up his motor and Bertie returned in triumph to bear Daisy and Amy off to London.

A thin, watery sunlight was struggling through the clouds to shine over the towers and spires of London Town when they putt-putted into Mayfair. The Duke, the cellar, the manor, the storm, all began to fade in Daisy's mind as if they had been part of some Gothic dream. Only the memory of the Duke's hard arms around her continued to nag at a small corner of her brain.

She found herself liking Bertie Burke immensely. He was admittedly naive and ingenuous, but by no means the silly ass he was reported to be.

With his weak, trusting eyes and narrow head, he reminded her of a friendly mongrel. And there was nothing to worry about in Bertie. No hidden passions, no jealousies, no resentments. Only a comfortable doglike and incoherent devotion emanated from him.

Although cricket bored her to death, Daisy cheerfully accepted an invitation to visit Lords with him on the following afternoon, and made her way thankfully to her bedroom in the Nottenstones' town house. That at least had the familiarity of a few weeks' occupation.

The Duke had surprisingly elected to stay on in Sussex and help the Countess salvage wines from the cellar. He had appeared briefly to say good-bye to Daisy with all his noted chilly indifference.

The Season drew to its exhausting close as Daisy began to enjoy herself for the first time in Bertie's undemanding company. He was always there when she needed an escort, happy as a puppy and as uncomplicated as a clear day.

The Earl and Countess of Nottenstone smiled on the relationship in public and joked about it in private. "What *on earth* can our little Daisy see in that chinless wonder," remarked Angela to her husband. "He's got money, of course, but that doesn't seem to have interested La Chatterton to date. Are we going to invite him to Brinton?" The Nottenstones had a villa at Brinton, a fashionable seaside resort on the south coast. "Why not?" said the Earl. "I can hear him now. 'Oh, I say.

Definitely. Absolutely. How jolly. How ripping. Oh, definitely.' "

"Are we inviting Oxenden?" asked Angela, becoming suddenly interested in a papier-mâché powder box.

The Earl gave her a quick look. "Well, we usually do. Though I can't see why he accepts. I would swear that man despises us."

"He despises all of us," said Angela lightly. "Then we'll ask him. And who else?"

"Don't know. Someone who is a bit of fun. Clive Fraser's a good sport. And what about Ann Gore-Brookes?"

"What about her, tee-hee?" said his wife maliciously.

"Oh, you're always sneering at her. But she's a good sport. Got a good seat on a horse."

"What on earth has that got to do with it?" said Angela pettishly. "Oh, ask who you want."

Bertie replied to the invitation in the manner expected of him, but did something that no one in London society would have credited him with having the courage to do.

He went to see his father.

Sir Gerald Burke lived in an enormous Palladian mansion in Berkshire, entirely alone—that is, if you discounted a whole army of servants. In an age of eccentrics he still managed to be outstanding. He shared his meals in the enormous dining room with his horse, and the horse and he often sat through the long reaches of the night sharing the port decanter, Sir Gerald with a heavy silver goblet, the horse with a flower bowl. The beautiful cornices, mouldings, and wainscoting were peppered with shot. He had a horror of bugs and would let fly with a blast at a cockroach with enough shot to paralyze a whole warren of rabbits. He was immensely rich, but even the most determined of toadies and gold diggers had ceased to call. If a fly buzzed over the dinner table, Sir Gerald would seize his gun and blast off in all directions. There had been, in the past, several distressing accidents, although the horse remained miraculously unharmed.

Sir Gerald was also famous for his frequent choleric rages, when he ran through his mansion dismissing all the staff. But since he could never remember any of their faces, they simply rehired themselves the next day. Unemployment in England was at a peak and the servants would rather take their chances of dying from a stray bullet than from starvation outside.

Bertie was terrified of him and hardly ever went near him. In fact, his father paid him a generous allowance to stay away.

"Hullo, hullo, McWhirter," said Bertie breezily, handing his hat and cane to the burly Scotch butler. "Father home?"

"Aye, that he is," said McWhirter gloomily. "But it's a rare fine day for the flies. Ye'd be better to leave, Mr. Bertie."

A sound of a shot reverberated around the hall. "There you are," said McWhirter with a kind of gloomy relish. "Flies."

"Oh, don't worry about me," said Bertie with an airiness he was far from feeling. "I grew up with it, you know. Well, here goes."

He strode into the drawing room and promptly dived under a coffee table as another blast nearly punctured his eardrums.

His father's scarlet and broken-veined face appeared upside down in Bertie's range of vision. "What'ye doin' under there?"

"Saving my life," said Bertie, getting up and brushing down his trousers.

The French windows were standing open showing a summer vista of rose arbors and cool green lawns. Bertie had a sudden impulse to take to his heels and run, but the thought of Daisy kept him where he was. A bee was hesitating on the threshold of the windows. If it entered the room all conversation would be killed . . . and perhaps Bertie as well. He plunged in.

"Look here, father. I'm going to get married."

Sir Gerald actually put down his shotgun. "*You* . . ." he said slowly. "Married?" Then he began to laugh with great wheezy gulps until he sank down exhausted on the chesterfield. "Who's the gel?" asked Sir Gerald when he could speak.

"The Honorable Daisy Chatterton."

"Chatterton!" howled Sir Gerald. "How dare

you, sir. How dare you try to drag down the name of Burke by marrying some cardsharp's bitch."

"Oh, I say," bleated Bertie.

"The Madeira, sir," said McWhirter at his elbow.

"You—what's your name?" roared Sir Gerald.

"Grange, sir," replied the butler. Every time he was fired, McWhirter changed his name and rehired himself.

"Don't dare interrupt me when I'm havin' a family powwow, or you'll end up in the street with all them other cheeky butlers."

"Very good, sir," said McWhirter, relieved that he would not have to think of a change of name for the time being anyway.

"Now, look here," said Sir Gerald. "You marry that gel and I'll cut you off without a penny."

"Then cut me off," said Bertie, made coolheaded by desperation. "I'll earn my living."

"Pah! Utter twaddle. Earn your living, you spineless fool. At what?"

"I'll become a cardsharp," said Bertie, studying his nails. "I'd better hoof off to France and ask her pater for some lessons. Then," he replied, warming to the subject, "I'll set up a house in London and call it Burke's Baccarat . . . no, no, Burke's Bohemia . . . or maybe Burke's . . ."

"Burke's Backside's more like it," snarled his parent. "You wouldn't anyway."

Bertie had burned his bridges and felt about ten feet tall. "Oh, yes I would, you horrible old man. And the only thing I'll take from you are a few photographs of yourself to terrify m'children."

He marched to the door, but was stopped by the sound of his father's voice, "I'll double your allowance."

"You'll *what*?"

"You heard me. Never thought to hear you standin' up to me. Gel's made a man out of you. Got m'blessing."

Bertie's sentimental soul was touched. He was about to stay and thank his parent in the warmest terms possible, but the bee made a suicidal lunge into the room. Before his father could reach the shotgun, Bertie was out of the room and running hard. Just wait till he told Daisy!

It was then he remembered that he hadn't even proposed.

Everything from the government to the Boers had been blamed for the freakish unseasonal summer that year, but as Daisy's train steamed into Brinton it seemed as if all the year's storms, fogs, and clouds had rolled away, leaving nothing but an endless blue, pristine sky. The small station was set on a rise above the town and as Daisy waited on the platform for the arrival of the carriages, she was able to see the whole of the resort spread out at her feet.

The old town huddled at one corner of the cove as if crouching at the feet of the aristocratic villas which lay spaced along the long line of the beach. The sea was as blue and as perfect as a painting, with little white sails dotted here and there on the horizon.

There was a fresh scent of pine and roses mingled with the smells of new-baked bread and strong tea from the stationmaster's cottage.

The villas were set back behind a row of white sandy dunes topped with sharp razor grass, looking in the distance like tiny strokes of an artist's brush.

Daisy stood enchanted, feeling the warmth of the sun through her striped cotton blouse and the light breeze tugging at her boater.

"You look most awfully pretty." It was Bertie at her elbow. Daisy turned and smiled at him indulgently, the way one does at the friendly importuning of a pet dog.

"Thank you, Bertie. Oh, look at that darling little cottage over there." Bertie sighed and looked and then looked at Daisy again. He tried to work up his courage to make another gallant remark, but Daisy was now in ecstasies over a row of brightly painted bathing machines. She had never seen the sea before. Could she bathe? Would the water be cold? Of course Bertie would know. And Bertie puffed out his thin chest and answered her questions and felt like a god.

It was a cheerful, frivolous party which finally debouched from the carriages outside the Nottenstones' villa. It was more of a mansion with wooden balconies and towers and a long colonnaded terrace running along the front of the house.

The Earl and Countess, when informed that the Duke of Oxenden had already arrived, looked at each other in some surprise. "Really, my dear," said Angela to her husband. "We must have charms we did not know of." She gave a silly little laugh and blushed and her husband colored angrily, and pinched the bottom of the between-stairs maid as soon as ever he could.

Daisy, Bertie, and Amy went off to explore the town and the little pier. When Bertie was hanging over the pier to see if he could spot any fish, Daisy put a halfpenny in a machine called What the Butler Saw and began to crank the handle. She took her head away from the machine with her face flaming. Those had been photographs. That meant a real live woman had taken off most of her clothes in front of a photographer. How on earth could anyone. . . ? Then she remembered her adventure in the cellar and felt an unmaidenly pang of regret. She would never be on such terms of intimacy with the handsome Duke again. She had met him briefly on the stairs and had been treated to his best bow. Bertie had been treated in exactly the same way. But Bertie had merely laughed and called the Duke a stuffed shirt.

They pottered about the shops stocked with musical boxes made of shells, brightly colored postcards, and buckets and spades. Little eddies of sand twisted over the cobbles of the main street. Somewhere in one of the flats over the shops a child was thumping out "Nola" on the piano, an old man was selling whelks and cockles from a barrow with a sign that read PLEASE RETURN PINS in curly script, and at the corner of the street the town drunk was roaring out "Bobbing Up and Down Like This" to the vast entertainment of a group of street urchins.

Bertie bought them a bag of whelks, but Amy ate the most. Daisy extracted one small creature with her pin and popped it into her mouth, but it tasted like salted rubber. Amy had stopped "walking out" with her young man some weeks before and now her large brilliant eyes were ever on the flirtatious alert for fresh game. She popped the shellfish into her mouth, tossing back her long curls and giving many sidelong glances toward a group of young men on the corner.

Bertie whispered to Daisy, "I say, Daisy, can't you keep that maid of yours under control? She's attracting the attention of that group of mashers."

Daisy began to explain that Amy was really more of a friend than a maid, but the sharp Amy had already caught Bertie's reproving look and immediately became the epitome of the respectable lady's maid, freezing the mashers with a disdainful stare.

Harmony restored, the threesome headed down to the beach and all social conventions were forgotten as they became schoolchildren again, searching for shells and ferreting in the small rock pools. Bertie had never been happier in his life. He was alone—well, nearly alone—with the girl he loved on this jolly beach, with no horrible society peers around to poke fun at him and make him feel like a fool.

With his hair hanging over his eyes, he gazed at Daisy with utter devotion and Daisy thought for the hundredth time how like a nice dog he looked and longed to scratch him behind the ears.

Sandy and happy, they rolled back to the villa in time for tea.

Angela and the Duke were seated alone at a white cane table in the garden. The Duke was impeccable in blazer and flannels and Angela managed to look incredibly seductive in a loose, flowing tea gown of sulphur yellow with a pattern of bronze flag iris. One of her long sleeves trailed over the Duke's arm. Daisy could not remember seeing him more amused and felt dusty and grubby.

"There you are, my children," cried Angela. "Leave your buckets and spades in the hall and go upstairs this minute and wash behind your ears."

She then turned and looked full into the Duke's eyes, cleverly establishing an intimacy that did not exist. Her husband, who had been about to join them, caught the look and retreated into the house instead where he bestowed a golden guinea on the buxom betweenstairs maid in the hope of favors yet to be received.

Daisy dressed for dinner with elaborate care, in a scarlet- and black-striped dinner gown, cut very low on the bosom, with enormous frilled and ruched sleeves. There was to be dancing after dinner and Angela had hired the minstrel band from the pier especially for the occasion. *Perhaps,* Daisy thought, *she would feel the Duke's arm around her again.*

But it seemed that the only arms she was going to feel about her were Bertie's. With no little irritation she noticed that everyone expected them to spend their time together. Really, how could one take Bertie seriously? And the Duke, noticing Bertie's shining face and shining eyes, hoped that Daisy knew what she was doing.

A little dance platform had been raised under some weeping willows beside an ornamental pool. A willow pattern bridge spanned the pool and Japanese lanterns were strung through the trees.

Ann Gore-Brookes was wearing an elaborate kimono and the Honorable Clive Fraser, a quilted mandarin coat. He had waxed his mustaches into two long curves, but little tendrils of luxuriant British mustache kept escaping, so that he looked as if he had two hairy caterpillars crawling up either side of his mouth.

Bertie, much to Daisy's mortification, had decided to appear as that well-known aristocratic tramp of the music hall, Burlington Bertie. His evening dress was flawless, his silk hat shining, but his fingers were sticking out of his gloves and his toes out of his shoes. And he had a monocle stuck in his eye. Daisy was just beginning to wonder whether or not she should be in fancy dress when the Duke appeared, impeccably elegant in formal evening dress. Angela was hanging on to his arm, a vision, in pale-gold tulle of a deceptively modest cut. Daisy felt overdressed and blowsy in comparison.

The Duke disengaged himself from Angela and crossed to Daisy's side at a moment when Bertie was talking to the band. "I think your young man is about to perform for us," remarked the Duke.

"He's *not* my young man," said Daisy crossly.

"Then may I point out that you are giving him a great deal of encouragement. While you are going 'round searching for true love, you seem to be forgetting that someone might fall in love with you and get badly hurt in the process."

"*Bertie!*" said Daisy in amazement. "Don't be so silly. Why, just look at him."

Bertie had launched into the opening lines of his song:

> *"I'm Burlington Bertie*
> *I rise at 10:30*
> *And go for a walk down the Strand . . ."*

The Duke smiled down at her. "Remember, Daisy, that the soul of Pagliacci may beat beneath the boiled shirt of the most correct young Englishman."

Bertie reached the end of his song:

> *"Nearly everyone knows me*
> *From Smith to Lord Roseberry*
> *I'm Burlington Bertie from Bow."*

Loud applause greeted his efforts and Bertie rushed immediately to Daisy's side. "What did you think, Daisy? Was I all right?"

"Yes yes" snapped Daisy in the manner of a mother whose child has tugged at her skirt for attention once too often. "Now you will be able to take off your hat and those terrible gloves."

Bertie looked crestfallen. "Suppose I look a bit of a fool, what? Sorry, Daisy."

"What for?" said Daisy cruelly. "What you do has nothing to do with me, Bertie Burke."

The Duke had just wandered off with the Countess. Her dress flickered like a pale flame in the darkness and then disappeared under the trees.

Daisy had an overwhelming desire to spy on them. Bertie had shuffled off and no one else seemed to be looking at her. Not stopping to analyze her motive, she slipped off into the darkness. Angela was wearing a very heavy, musky perfume which wafted across on the still night air, mingling with the faint tang of salt from the sea. She was so intent on her pursuit that she nearly stumbled into them. Angela's white arms were wound around the Duke's neck and he was kissing her. Daisy gave a little cry and turned and ran off back to the dance.

She felt immeasurably hurt and could not understand why. *The Duke has no right to philander with a married woman,* she thought savagely. She had underrated the affections of poor Bertie. She would show the Duke of Oxenden that she did not care a rap. By the time he returned to the dance floor, Daisy was flirting outrageously with Bertie, who looked as if all his dreams had just come true. Daisy was just leaning forward to take a sip of wine from Bertie's glass when she was suddenly jerked onto the dance floor by a strong arm.

She stared at the Duke's waistcoat, breathless and shy, and aware of his eyes staring down at the top of her head. He began without preamble: "I have been kissed by Angela before and it means absolutely nothing to me. Or to her for that matter. But your case is different. I would advise you not to flirt so assiduously with that young man, unless you mean to marry him."

"Marry! Marry *Bertie,*" laughed Daisy. "You must be mad."

"Look, Daisy, I warn you . . ."

"*You* warn *me.*" Daisy broke away from him. "Let me tell you, my lord Duke, you are not my father and I shall do exactly as I please."

Trembling with rage, she walked away from him and joined Bertie who threw the Duke a triumphant look. "Let's get away from them for a bit, Daisy," he said. "Let's go for a stroll on the beach."

Daisy gladly agreed. Anything to get away from the Duke's angry stare and Angela's mocking eyes.

They climbed up over the dunes and stood together for a moment, looking down on the beach. The water was still and quiet like black glass, with only a thin white line of foam moving on the empty beach. A long line of light from the lighthouse stabbed across the bay. Daisy stood silently, breathing in the peace of the night and idly counting the flashes of light.

"Let's go down on the beach," said Bertie. "There's something I must say." Daisy smiled vaguely and moved slowly along beside him over the dunes, the stiff taffeta of her petticoats making a steady whish-whishing sound like the incoming tide. Probably Bertie wanted to discuss another of his many plans for her amusement.

They walked side by side to the edge of the water and stood looking down at the little waves curling gently over the sand. Daisy burst out laughing. "Whatever are you doing, Bertie, kneeling on the sand like that? You'll ruin your trousers."

Bertie stared up at her, his face glistening with sweat in the moonlight. "Daisy, will you marry me?"

Daisy stepped back in alarm. She had an absurd desire to say, "This is so sudden." Instead she blurted out, "Oh, Bertie. Stop acting the fool and let's get back to the party."

"I mean it, Daisy," said Bertie slowly and earnestly. "You're the prettiest gel I've ever seen. Honest. I'm most awfully, terribly in love with you."

Daisy shook her head slowly in a wondering way. This could not possibly be *Bertie* proposing to her.

He rose to his feet and flung his arms around her and tried to kiss her. His whole body was trembling, his breath smelled of wine and cigars, and she could feel his damp, cold hands on her shoulders. She wrenched her face away and found herself stammering, "P-please, B-Bertie. Leave me *alone*. I didn't think you were serious. *Please* leave me alone. I can't feel anything for you."

"But you must. You *must*!" babbled Bertie. He sank to his knees again and buried his face in her skirts. She wrenched her dress away and he stayed, kneeling on the sands, his head bent. Bertie felt his heart break and Daisy felt as if some pet dog had suddenly gone into heat and started making love to her foot.

"I'm leaving, Bertie," she said, starting to move away. "You've had a bit too much to drink, that's it. You'll see things quite differently in the morning."

Bertie began to cry. Great, racking sobs shook his thin body and the ugly, choking sounds filled the still night air.

Daisy made a half move toward him and then abruptly turned and ran headlong up the beach. She did not stop running until she had reached the safety of her bedroom and poured the whole story into Amy's ears.

"He must have been drunk, Amy" she wailed.

Amy shook her head slowly. "He's awfully keen on you, Daisy. I thought to warn you but then you seemed to like his company and went everywhere with him . . . well, be honest, Daisy. You did give the poor chap a lot of encouragement."

"How—how was I to *know*," cried Daisy.

"I think," said Amy, "that you're so keen on finding love for yourself, that you forget that someone might be falling in love with you. Where did you leave him?"

"On the beach."

Amy wound a shawl around her blonde hair. "I'd better go and make sure he does nothing silly."

"Silly!" cried Daisy. The weight of guilt within her seemed already too heavy to bear.

"There, there," said Amy. "The damage is done and there is nothing more you can do. I'll go."

Daisy sat miserably by the window for a long time after Amy had left. Up till now, her life had seemed very unreal and the various people she met, merely players in it. There was no one else to blame but herself. Hot tears of shame began to burn down her cheeks. She had a longing to see the father she had never known. She would go to France. Nothing would stop her now.

* * *

Her white shawl flying about her shoulders like wings, Amy fled through the sleeping town of Brinton. The beach had been deserted, but heavy footprints had marked a stumbling path up and over the dunes to the shore road. The cobbles of the town shone in the moonlight, a stray cat made a sudden dash across the road, but apart from that, no other figures moved. Amy was just about to give up the search when she remembered the pier.

The long white sanded boards stretched out into the bay. The flags at the entrance hung motionless in the still air. The slot machines stood against the rail on their squat legs, like some fantastic army lined up for review. Amy ran lightly along the pier, her slippered feet making no sound on the boards, past the theater where the coming attraction of "Romeo and Juliet" featuring that well-known actor, Bertram Dufresne, was billed in large ornate letters, and out to the platform at the end.

Bertie Burke stood at the very edge, his forehead pressed against a post and his thin chest heaving with great sobs. Amy did not find Bertie in the least ridiculous. She was happily at home in the English caste system and Mr. Burke was a gentleman.

Moving gently so as not to frighten him, Amy said very quietly, "What are you doing out here, Mr. Burke?"

He turned around. Seen through a mist of tears, with her white shawl, and the moonlight shining on her blonde curls, Amy looked like a vision.

Then he blinked his eyes and registered that the vision was none other than Daisy's maid. His humiliation was complete.

Pulling himself together with pathetic dignity, he said, "I'm about to make a great, big hole in the water."

"You'd be very much missed," said Amy, moving cautiously as close to him as she dared.

Bertie looked at her with contempt. "Who'd miss me? Daisy?"

"Well, now, I suppose she would. She ain't in love with you. But she likes you a lot."

Bertie began to cry again. He tried valiantly to stop, but seemed unable to.

"Then there's all your friends," said Amy. "Oh, I know they tease you a bit. But they'd miss you. Why, only the other day I heard his lordship, the Earl, say, 'That Bertie always makes me laugh. He's a jolly good sport.'"

Bertie wiped his weak eyes with a sodden handkerchief and looked at her suspiciously, but Amy went on, "You see, you're always so merry and the life and soul of any party, that people don't think you've got feelings same as them. Us cheery ones always get the sticky end. Take me now . . . I was walking out with a fellow and we had an understanding like. Then he starts on as how he wants to be a butler and how nobody recognizes his worth . . . on and on he'd go. I'd try to sympathize and say I understood and he'd sneer at me and say 'How can you understand the feelings of a chap what wants to make his mark in the world? You're always laughing. Always got a cheery word. You don't know how to suffer.' Well, maybe I don't. But I don't go around making everyone else miserable and taking myself too seriously, if that's what he means by suffering."

She had moved next to Bertie and now put a hand on his arm. "But you get it off your chest. Doesn't do to suffer in silence. Just take it very quietly and tell Amy. There now." She put a comforting arm around his narrow shoulders and held him until his sobbing ceased.

He gave a tired little hiccup and sigh like a small child, and began to speak: "Well, you see, it's like this. I'm most awfully, terribly in love and she's such a ripping girl . . ."

A little breeze began to wrinkle the water, the moon slid down the sky, and still the two figures stood at the end of the pier, the man talking earnestly and the blonde girl holding him as tightly as a mother holds an injured child.

Chapter Twelve

The next morning the sun blazed down from a brassy sky and the air was heavy, still, and humid. The gardener weeding the flower beds was the only moving thing on the immediate horizon. The Earl and Countess of Nottenstone were breakfasting on the terrace. Their guests were still in bed although it was eleven in the morning. The heat was already suffocating and definitely un-English.

Angela threw down her fork and picked up her fan and started flapping it angrily.

"I'm bored, bored, *bored,*" she said petulantly. "Why did we have to come to this boring bourgeois place anyway? It positively reeks of aspidistras and Low Anglicans. Why didn't we go to Trouville with everyone else?"

"I don't know," said the Earl sleepily. "You liked it well enough last year."

The year before, the Earl and Countess had bought the villa at the height of one of their more dramatic reconciliations.

"Or Paris," went on Angela. "Paris is *such* fun. Do you remember when the Comte de Leon was racing his carriage down the Avenue du Bois and knocked that silly little man over who started shouting 'Murderer! Murderer!' and the Comte simply took out one of those old-fashioned green-silk purses that ladies used to carry—absolutely weighted down with gold—and threw it in the fellow's face? *So Balzacky,*" she sighed. "Now, there was a *man.*"

"Implying that I am not," said the Earl icily, putting down his beer tankard.

"Don't pout," said his wife maddeningly, looking more cheerful now that she had succeeded in upsetting him.

"And furthermore," snapped her husband, "the comte and the rest of them are degenerates, always fathering each other's children and creeping around each other's bedrooms and living in each other's pockets."

"You know, you really are a rather ghastly Victorian. The old Queen must have loved you. I'm sure Neddy thinks you're a stuffed shirt."

"Are you by any chance referring to the King in that familiar manner or do you mean Daisy Chatterton's father?"

"That ghastly old tottering drip? No, my precious darling, I mean Kingie."

"His Highness has always been all that is pleasant."

"Exactly," sneered his wife. "If Kingie didn't

think you were a stuffed shirt, he'd take you out roistering with him."

"King Edward does not roister."

"Hah!" remarked the Countess with Palmerstonian venom. "What *is* up with you, Davy? What little piece of merriment have you planned for us all today?"

The Earl gazed out over the oily sea. "The vicar and his wife are coming to tea."

"The vicar and—oh, you can't mean it. You've gone stark, raving mad. Have you started worrying about your immortal soul, my dear? Well, I agree with Mr. Darwin. We are all descended from chimps. But if you think I am going to stay home this afternoon listening to some dreary vicar's wife giving me her recipe for cauliflower—oh gracious, you can think again."

The Earl turned around in his high-backed cane chair and looked at her with eyes as flat and expressionless as the flat, summer sea. "You will stay to meet the vicar. You will do the pretty to Mrs. Vicar. I am weary of this racketing around. Oxenden was the last straw."

"*Toby*. What has Toby got to do with it?"

"Oxenden breaks hearts whether he means to or not," said the Earl. "He's heavy stuff. Now, you will start behaving like the Countess of Nottenstone and not like some *demi-mondaine*, or you can pack your bags and get out."

She opened her mouth to reply, but Ann Gore-Brookes rushed in and dragged a chair up to the table with much scraping and scratching. She was obviously bursting with news for her long nose was quite pink with excitement. "You'll never guess what," she began.

The married couple stared at her with disdain. She hesitated and then rushed on. "Bertie Burke is quite *bouleversé* with love over that Daisy-girl. Fact, darlings, the second footman, George, was returning along the shore road late last night when we were all at the dance and Bertie dashes past him with tears running down his face and sobbing like the Mock Turtle and saying he's going to end it all and nobody loves him."

"And the second footman no doubt rushed to your arms to tell you," said Angela coldly.

Ann Gore-Brookes bridled. "Of course not. He told my maid and my maid told me."

The Earl rang a small handbell on the table. "Ah, Curzon," he said to the butler. "Would you please ascertain whether Mr. Burke has committed suicide or not."

"Very good, my lord."

Curzon went off and left the three to sit in silence. Ann was insulted, Angela shocked over her husband's threat, and the Earl was burning with a slow, smoldering anger.

In a few minutes Curzon was back. "Mr. Burke is still very much of this world, my lord," he said. "He asked me if we had kippers and said he would like two large ones served with strawberry jam."

"There you are," said Angela with forced jollity. "He's going to kill himself a bit at a time, starting with his stomach. What do you think Bertie's stomach is like anyway? I imagine it as being slightly flabby and covered with a thin film of sweat and . . ."

"*Go to your room,*" roared the Earl.

Angela stared at her husband. Ann Gore-Brookes let out a nervous tee-hee and Curzon withdrew behind a wisteria-draped column.

The Duke of Oxenden strolled languidly into the scene. Angela stretched out an appealing hand toward him. "Oh, Toby. Davy has just ordered me to my room. Just as if I were a naughty child or something. He . . ."

"Then why don't you go?" remarked the Duke with bored indifference.

Angela gave a choking sob and fled.

Daisy stayed hiding in her room, breakfast-less and luncheon-less until, by the time the tea gong rang, she could bear it no longer. Amy had assured her that Bertie had recovered, but she still felt ashamed and guilty.

Her entrance onto the lawn where everyone was assembled around a table under the willows was something of an anticlimax. No one—not even Bertie—looked around at her. All attention was focused on Angela, Countess of Nottenstone. She was dressed in a cheap cotton-print gown with a high frill at the neck and long, tight sleeves. Her hair was scraped painfully from her forehead and screwed in a bun at the back. She had hung several crucifixes around her neck and placed the Bible and the Book of Common Prayer conspicuously beside the Queen Anne silver teapot.

"Now don't you think I look the part?" teased Angela, grinning at the Duke. The Earl seemed to be almost immobilized with fury.

His Grace looked at her thoughtfully from under drooping lids. "My dear Angela," he said finally. "Members of the Church of England are not always as unworldly as you seem to think. Your own vicar is quite the sophisticate."

"Dear Percy," sighed Angela. "That's why we chose him. But *Brinton,* my dear Toby. They'll be terribly Low Church."

To add to her dowdy appearance, she had covered her face with a layer of gray powder. As soon as the vicar, the Reverend Peter Blessop, and Mrs. Blessop were announced, she cast down her eyes and folded her hands in her lap.

The vicar turned out to be a mild and courtly gentleman in his forties, wearing a shabby but respectable New College blazer and white flannels. His pale blue, myopic eyes looked around the guests like a pleased child and he actually clapped his hands when he saw the tea table. "Plum cake!" he cried with a high, fluting voice. "What a treat. I cannot remember when we last had plum cake. Now let me see . . . was it at little Johnny Spencer's christening or was it when Jean Barrington-French got married to that captain in the Life-guards . . . ?"

He rambled on but no one was paying him the least attention. All eyes were fixed on his wife. Mrs. Blessop was in her early twenties and with all the startling beauty of a Dresden figurine. Her golden curls rioted over her small head in artless profusion, her complexion was a miracle of peaches and cream, and her tea gown was in the latest fashion.

Angela looked as if she had suddenly discovered an extra slice of lemon in her tea, the Honorable Clive was fingering his mustache, the Earl was leaping about to procure a chair for the beauty, and even Bertie Burke looked as if the sun had just risen over a particularly gloomy horizon.

"So pleased to meet you, my lady," said Mrs. Blessop in a soft, babyish voice. "I have heard so much of your beauty that . . ." her voice trailed away and she stared at her teacup. It was beautifully done. It was only long afterward that Daisy discovered that Mrs. Blessop had been a promising young actress at the Haymarket Theater. Angela glared and remarked, "I think of higher things than clothes, my dear Mrs. Blessop. I may not be in my customary looks today, but I think that one should occasionally devote one's time to more spiritual things."

"Oh, indeed," sighed Mrs. Blessop, pouting prettily. "I am afraid you will find me a very shallow creature, my lady. I do so love pretty clothes and parties and—and—you don't mind if I say this, do you Peter, darling—the company of all these *handsome* gentlemen."

The handsome gentlemen beamed upon her with the exception of the Duke who merely looked quietly amused.

"Now, of course, there is my sister Edna. She's terribly plain and has a wart on the end of her nose. It's so easy for her to keep to the straight and narrow path because, you see, no one ever wants to lead her from it. And she wears these terrible gowns, print cottons, my dears, and—" She looked at the Countess's gown, blushed prettily, and stared in confusion at her hands. That Angela was seething was quite obvious to everyone and most were delighted. There is nothing more delicious than to sit on a beautiful lawn on an English summer's day and comfortably survey the mortification of one of your best friends. But Daisy felt that someone ought to go to Angela's defense.

She gathered her courage and gave a little cough to catch everyone's attention. Daisy knew that her own tea gown was a miracle of sophistication straight from Paris, so she said, "I am extremely lucky. I do not have much dress sense myself, so I have to rely on her ladyship's impeccable taste. I follow her advice in everything. This Paris gown was entirely her inspiration."

Mrs. Blessop surveyed Daisy's gown for a few seconds. A flicker of something not quite holy flashed briefly in her eyes and then she said in her soft, carrying voice, "Oh, my dear, you are *so* lucky to be able to afford Paris gowns. Now I, I am only a poor vicar's wife and I made this poor little rag all by myself."

The Earl, Bertie, and the Honorable Clive immediately exclaimed in surprise, "though," as Clive Fraser put it, "you look so enchanting, my dear, that I believe you could wear a sack and still look divine."

"There you are, Angela," said her husband heartily. "Instead of costing me a fortune in gowns, you could be running them up yourself, what!"

Daisy found herself looking to Ann Gore-Brookes for help. As the only other lady of the party, it was surely her turn to say *something.*

Ann Gore-Brookes had no wit, so she fell back on that last bastion of the English upper classes. "What school did you go to?" she asked in a loud voice, pointing her long pink nose in Mrs. Blessop's direction.

"I didn't go to school," said Mrs. Blessop. "I was educated at home."

"Hah!" said Ann, moving in for the kill. "I think I've seen you somewhere before. What's your maiden name?"

"Higgins," said Mrs. Blessop softly.

"Higgins? Higgins? Never heard of them. Which county?"

Mrs. Blessop's blue eyes filled slowly with tears. "The Higginses of nowhere," she said sadly. "My mother and father were not anybody special, you see. That was why I was so amazed when a gentleman like Peter fell in love with me. 'You should not be ashamed of your background,' he told me. 'And if anyone tries to tease you about it, why then, they must be very insecure about their own.' "

Ann Gore-Brookes flushed an ugly color and retired defeated while the gentlemen made soothing noises. Ann's grandfather had been a Yorkshire button manufacturer and she immediately assumed that the horrid Mrs. Blessop had divined all. In fact, the shrewd Mrs. Blessop had discovered that almost all families had some sort of skeleton in their closet, after a short lifetime of parrying social snubs.

Her perfect performance—and by now Daisy was convinced that Mrs. Blessop was a consummate actress as well as a bitch on wheels—made Daisy think of the theater. To change the subject she asked if anyone would be going to see the performance of *Romeo and Juliet* in Brinton during the coming week. She had heard that Mr. Bertram Dufresne was a superb actor. The Earl, who was now giving Mrs. Blessop the benefit of his chiseled profile, said with a laugh that he didn't go in for all that "slushy nonsense."

Mrs. Blessop turned her brilliant eyes on the Earl and fluttered her beautiful hands. Daisy stared spellbound. Somehow for a few seconds, Mrs. Blessop *was* Angela. Every flirtatious movement was correct to an inch. Daisy suddenly felt that somehow, somewhere, sometime, Mrs. Blessop had seen and studied the Countess and knew that Angela's present dress and appearance were all part of an act.

"But you *must* go, your lordship. I will be there."

"Then in that case," grinned the Earl, "I'll certainly be there, too. We'll make up a party. What do you say, vicar?"

The vicar, who had been carrying on a low and intense conversation with Bertie, looked up and remarked vaguely, "Of course, of course. Anything you say," and went back to his conversation.

"Do you by any chance disapprove of the theater, my lady?" asked Mrs. Blessop.

"I do not disapprove of playacting, provided it is confined to the theater," said Angela waspishly. "It's getting late. Curzon, clear these things. It has been charming to meet you, Mrs. Blessop. *So* educational. It is not everyday that one meets someone with the courage not to be ashamed of their low beginnings and . . ."

"It's too early to hurry away," said the Earl. "I'll take you on a tour of the gardens and Angela, you can show Mr. Blessop the library."

Angela went quite pink with anger under her gray powder. She longed to go and change. But to do so would be to admit to this horrible vicar's wife that she had been playing a game. Then she wondered whether Mrs. Blessop could be made jealous. "Perhaps," she mused, "I *will* put on my prettiest gown, and to hell with what she thinks."

By the time everyone gathered in the drawing room for sherry, the air was electric. Mrs. Blessop looked like a cream-fed kitten, the Earl was radiant, and Angela was exhausted. Nothing had gone right. No dress seemed suitable. She had screamed at her maid until the nervous woman had burned the Countess's neck with the curling tongs. Angela had slapped her and had then tried to brand her with the tongs and the poor woman was only rescued by the arrival of Curzon who had firmly taken charge and directed operations, flattering Angela's damaged ego and managing to get her to wear one of her hundreds of gowns and to present herself in the drawing room at the appointed time.

She was looking very beautiful, but there was an impervious aura of power emanating from Mrs. Blessop, and with one look at her husband, Angela knew exactly what had caused it. She was sure nothing further than an intense flirtation had taken place, but that was heady stuff indeed for the vicar's wife. The vicar himself had refused Angela's tour of the library. Mr. Burke had a problem he wished to discuss, he had said with surprising firmness.

"Have some sherry, vicar," said the Earl. "I am sure you will find it excellent." He turned to his wife with a forgiving smile. "Don't you find it so, my dear?"

"It tastes," said Angela, "as if it has been drunk already."

The Duke of Oxenden gave a snort of laughter. Daisy realized suddenly that the Duke was perhaps too coolly amused by people. He never seemed to get involved, simply watching the action as if he were at a play. *That is why he never falls in love,* thought Daisy. *How can you fall in love if you remain a bystander the whole time?* She had an urge to tell him so and did when no one else was listening.

He looked down at her earnest face, a wicked yellow light dancing in his eyes. "Perhaps you should follow my example, my dear child. That way you would not drive young men to contemplating suicide."

Daisy flushed. "I think you're horrid."

"No, you don't, my dear goose. You are merely jealous of my lack of reaction."

She opened her mouth to reply, but was interrupted by a horrendous crash. The Countess had thrown the sherry decanter through the window.

The reason for her outburst, Mrs. Blessop, was crying and appealing to the gentlemen that she hadn't meant anything nasty. Angela had said to Mrs. Blessop, "As you can see, I am restored to my natural beauty."

"Oh, really," Mrs. Blessop had replied. "I had not noticed any difference, I can assure you, my lady."

For once, at a loss for a reply, Angela had

resorted to violence. To Daisy's amazement, the vicar was still talking earnestly to Bertie and did not bother to look up.

"Take me home, Peter," wailed Mrs. Blessop.

The vicar did look up then and blinked myopically around the room at the shattered window and the furious Countess. "Really, my dear," he said mildly. "I shall be ready in a few minutes. Dear me, another accident. You are a sort of jinx. I remember when we were at Mrs. Jean Barrington-French's the other day, the teapot mysteriously flew from her hand, quite by accident, and nearly hit you and then Mr. Barrington-French slapped her. This young generation. You are all too impulsive, my children."

The Countess flounced from the room and the rest of the impulsive children applied themselves feverishly to the fresh decanter of sherry which the unflappable Curzon had thoughtfully produced.

The Earl was helping Mrs. Blessop dry her tears. The theater outing was discussed and everyone agreed to go.

The heat in the drawing room had become intense, so they all drifted out to the garden. The great trees hung heavily over the lawns as though bowed down by the unexpected jungle heat.

Encased in the rigid formality of correct dress, the party stood about the lawns in their confines of stays and waistcoats, their faces turned searching for the breeze which never came.

Chapter Thirteen

By the time the theater evening arrived, nerves and tempers at the villa were frayed by the constant scenes between the Earl and Countess and the hot, unrelenting brassy weather.

The only person who seemed surprisingly calm and unmoved was Bertie. He had lost his earnest puppyish good humor, but he seemed more relaxed, and the Honorable Clive was able to report with awe that Bertie had been surprised in the library *reading a book.* For one dreadful moment all feared for his sanity and only breathed sighs of relief when the book turned out to be a *Guide to the Turf.*

Before the carriages were brought around, Daisy trailed down to the butler's pantry to search for Curzon.

She found him enjoying a glass of port in the stuffy cubicle. He was sitting minus his collar and jacket and seemed at peace with the world. They chatted away like old friends. Curzon often seemed to Daisy like the only human being in an artificial world. Apart from the fact that he inexplicably refused to discuss her father, he was reassuring and helpful on all other subjects. Bertie, he assured her, would not die of love. It was well known that Mr. Burke had been and still was bullied by his father. His mother had died when he was very young and Bertie was apt to put any young woman he was attracted to on a very high pedestal.

"He's the sort of young fellow who needs to marry out of his class," said Curzon. "I've seen some of 'em like that settling down with the local barmaid and living pretty happily ever after."

The rattle of the carriages outside interrupted their conversation and Daisy rose reluctantly to go. Mrs. Blessop was to be of the party and that promised another hideous evening of scenes between her host and hostess.

The air was suffocatingly close and hot and even at the end of the pier where the theater was housed in a wooden pentagon, no breath of air moved. It looked as if it was going to be a full house. The ladies languidly waved their fans to combat the heat and the gentlemen groaned in their prisons of stiff collars and evening jackets, tailored to fit as tightly as any of the ladies' stays.

The theater smelled of perfume, greasepaint, and sweat. Daisy began to wish she had stayed quietly at home with a book. The plush seats were very small and she was jammed between the Duke and Bertie. Mrs. Blessop's tinkling laugh—so like

Angela's—floated along the row toward her and the tension emitting from Angela was almost tangible.

When the shabby curtains parted Daisy sat forward in her chair and lost herself in Verona. From the moment that Mr. Bertram Dufresne strode on the stage in all the glory of a pair of pink tights and a sparkling silver doublet, Daisy was lost. He had a high, aquiline profile and a mop of black curly hair worn long on his shoulders. His accent was very slightly French. His Juliet was rather old and buxom for the part, but Daisy paid her not the slightest attention. Her eyes were all for Mr. Dufresne. When he spoke, he spoke for Daisy. When he died, he died for Daisy. She sat with the happy tears coursing down her cheeks as Shakespeare's famous tragedy came to a close.

The curtains parted again and several excited young ladies ran to the front of the theater and showered the romantic Mr. Dufresne with flowers. Daisy stared at him with her heart in her eyes. All thoughts of running away to France had fled. She would sit at Mr. Dufresne's feet for as long as she could.

Her party finally rose to leave with much shuffling and grumbling from the men and mutterings of "damned mountebank" from the Honorable Clive.

"I promised we would go backstage and meet the cast," said the Earl, "but it's just too damned hot."

"Oh, please," cried Daisy loudly, and then added shyly as the others turned to stare at her, "I've never been backstage in a theater before."

"It will only take a minute, David," said the Duke, surprisingly coming to her aid. "I suppose we just have to shake hands with them all and then we can leave."

Trembling with excitement and with her heart in her mouth, Daisy followed the others around to the stage door. The cast was lined up on the stage as if for a royal visit. Mrs. Blessop was not of the party, explaining that she felt unaccountably faint.

Daisy, moving down the row, well aware that Romeo was getting nearer every minute, tried to control her shaking hands. At last she was facing him and he was smiling down at her through his makeup. He saw before him one of the most beautiful debutantes he had ever seen. Daisy's soft brown hair was piled over her head, making her face seem very small and fragile. A white silk dress of deceptive simplicity clung to her hourglass figure and her large eyes were full of tremulous adoration.

He took a rose from the bouquet that Juliet was holding and presented it to Daisy with a magnificent bow. "Thank you," she whispered shyly and then became aware that there were other people behind her waiting to be presented. She moved along the line, shaking hands, and staring up at the glistening greasepainted faces, without really noticing any of them.

Afterward, when they were seated in the carriages and trotting sedately along the shore road to join a party at one of the neighboring mansions, Daisy sat dreamily clutching her rose.

When the dancing started later she danced around the floor with her feet scarcely seeming to touch the ground. Every partner was Romeo and the ballroom was in Verona. The Duke of Oxenden was well aware of it and found to his surprise that he was getting very angry indeed.

He could not be jealous, of course. He had never been jealous in his life before and the mere idea was ridiculous. He was only angry because this stupid little girl was about to go and make a fool of herself over some cardboard actor. Perhaps she *would* be better off with her father. The man was a fraud and a cheat, but he was her father and daughters seemed to love the most impossible parents. A plan began to form in his head. He would supply her with her father's address and then make sure she was suitably chaperoned. Daisy would find out that the generous allowance she was receiving through Curzon did not come from her father, but he would cope with that when the time came.

He drew her aside and had to repeat what he was saying several times in order to get through Daisy's magic world. She grasped the piece of paper with the address on it, put it in her reticule, smiled a vague "thank you," and moved off to dance with someone else.

With supreme irritation he noticed that she was wearing Romeo's rose at her bosom.

Amy was horrified when Daisy poured out her tale of the theater, before going to bed.

"Actors!" cried Amy raising her hands in horror. "They're not respectable, Daisy. Not respectable at all. A real riffraff bunch, if you ask me."

"Well, I'm not all that respectable myself, it seems to me," said Daisy.

"Now, then, Dais', your auntie or whatever she was may have been a bit strict, but she brought you up proper. What on earth would Miss Sarah Jenkins say if she knew you was running after an actor."

Both began to giggle as they knew exactly what Miss Jenkins would have said.

"Could you come with me tomorrow night to the theater, Amy?" pleaded Daisy, when they had stopped laughing.

"It's my night off tomorrow," said Amy. "I can't. I'm seeing a fellow."

"Oh, Amy," cried Daisy, momentarily diverted. "Who is it? Is it that nice young footman with the curly hair?" But Amy refused to be drawn out. She promised to accompany Daisy any other night and left it at that.

Daisy went happily to sleep with her precious rose beside her on her pillow.

In the morning, however, the idea of missing

a whole evening without seeing her Romeo seemed impossible. In despair, she asked Bertie to escort her and, to her surprise, heard herself being firmly turned down. Bertie, it seemed, had other plans. In fact, he had lost his hangdog look and seemed indecently cheerful.

With some trepidation, Daisy approached the Duke. Almost waspishly, he reminded her that they were all going to a party at a nearby country house and added that he refused to waste his time viewing a pack of indifferent actors for the second time. Any glimpses of warmth or affection toward her had disappeared and Daisy felt unaccountably friendless. Curzon, when appealed to, turned out to hold the same strong views against actors as Amy.

Daisy was in despair. She could not go unescorted to a public theater. She was interrupted in her dismal thoughts by the Earl who asked her if she would like to take a turn around the garden.

"I gather you are quite stagestruck," he said in a fatherly voice that sounded odd, coming as it did from his young and handsome face. Daisy nodded dumbly and then burst out about how much she wanted to visit the theater again, but that she had no one to escort her.

The Earl poked a flower bed with his cane and keeping his face turned away from her, he said in a muffled voice, "I know what it means to you, Daisy. I used to be a bit stagestruck myself. I tell you what, I'll take you along tonight," and interrupting her cry of gratitude, "but I ain't sitting through the whole thing again. I'll see you to your seat and when the show starts I'll nip outside for a cigar. And then I'll come back again just before it finishes. That way no one will know you're alone."

"What about the party?" asked Daisy.

"We can drive on afterward," he said cheerfully. "Angela won't mind. She ain't speaking to me."

Their proposed visit to the theater was received indifferently by the rest of the house party, with the exception of the Duke who felt he would like to punch the Earl and then shake Miss Daisy Chatterton till her teeth rattled.

Daisy sailed through the day on a pink cloud. As she was dressing with unusual care for the evening, Angela appeared at the doorway of her room carrying a long leather box.

"You're in love with Mr. Dufresne," she said boldly. Daisy blushed and shook her head, but Angela only laughed. "Well, my dear, I know you will want to look your dazzling best, so I thought you might like to borrow these." She flicked back the lid of the box and Daisy stared down at one of the most beautiful diamond necklaces she had ever seen.

"I—I couldn't possibly wear them," she stammered. "I should be terrified . . ."

"Nonsense, this is a very law-abiding community and Davy will be with you. I don't mind him going, by the way, he's just trying to annoy me."

Again Daisy shook her head. Angela moved

closer and held the box under Daisy's eyes. "Think of it, Daisy," she whispered. "You can't really see faces across the footlights, but his eyes will be caught by these and *then* he will see you. Look how they shine." She tilted the box backward and forward in the gaslight and the myriad colors flashed before Daisy's hypnotized eyes. "See," said Angela gently, "I'll just leave them on your dressing table. Enjoy your evening, my dear."

Daisy longed to wear the diamonds, but suspected a trap. Perhaps Angela was jealous of her for going out with her husband and wished Daisy somehow to lose the jewels so that she could be disgraced. She consulted Amy and Amy consulted Curzon. The butler said the jewels were not a family heirloom, although they were magnificent, and that they were heavily insured. He suspected that the Countess was simply being as nice as possible to make the Earl feel guilty.

The diamonds seemed to hypnotize Amy as well. "Put them on, Dais'," she urged. "It's just for one evening after all. Hurry, there's a dear. I've got to run to meet my young man."

Daisy put the six strands of heavy, cold diamonds around her neck where they blazed on her bosom like fire. She was wearing a dress of scarlet chiffon and the jewels picked out the color and flashed little red sparks around the room.

The Earl did not seem surprised when he saw the necklace. "Angela has these generous outbursts from time to time," he explained. "She's too lazy to plot."

Back again in the dark, dusty warmth of the theater, Daisy and the Earl sat in the front row, oblivious of the attention the diamonds caused, the Earl because he was used to being noticed and Daisy, because her heart was already in Verona. When the Earl rose to leave Daisy did not even notice him going. She did not notice him returning at the end of the performance, either, for Romeo had noticed her! He looked across the footlights into her eyes—really looked at her when he took his curtain call. A note was pressed into her hands by a messenger. As the houselights went up, she opened it and read *Please come to the Green Room. I must see you. Your Romeo.*

Daisy's heart beat fast. Would the Earl allow her to go? But the Earl, who was reeking of port and good humor, said that of course she could go and he would accompany her.

"What is the Green Room?" asked Daisy as they moved out into the warm, heavy night air.

"It's just a room where the actors gather to meet people at the back of the stage," said the Earl. "Don't be long, Daisy. We're expected to join the others soon."

The Green Room was actually furnished in several shades of dingy red and brown. Still in his costume, Romeo sat on a sofa, looking a dramatic and renaissance figure by the light of one small candle.

"Don't you have gaslight here?" asked Daisy, moving forward nervously.

"I'm afraid they reserve the luxuries for the front of the house," said Mr. Dufresne in his slight French accent. The Earl wandered around in the shadows, examining pieces of costume.

"I wished to see you again, Miss Chatterton. Ah, you see! I remember your name. Can he hear us?" He pointed to the Earl. Daisy whispered, "I don't think so. Why?"

"Because I wish to tell you that I love you," he said in a low voice. "I hope you do not think it forward of me."

There was a rustling in the darkness and a faint giggle. "Clowns," he said bitterly. "I had hoped we would be alone but, in my profession, there are always jealous actors about."

He took her hand and she felt a thrill go through her body like an electric shock.

"Come tomorrow night. Come alone," he whispered. Daisy gazed at the silver figure of Romeo and felt enchanted. They seemed to be locked away together in the circle of candlelight, from the petty world around.

"I will come tomorrow," she said softly, moving toward the door. He bent over and kissed her hand and then gazed into her eyes. "I have never loved any woman the way I love you," he said simply.

"I—I—I—love you too," said Daisy in a choked whisper.

The Earl joined them and said a few pleasant

commonplaces to Mr. Dufresne and then led Daisy from the theater.

When Daisy and the Earl arrived at the party the guests were already playing charades and the room was in darkness. The only person to notice Daisy's shining face and shining jewels was the Duke, who felt suddenly liverish and decided to go home.

That night Amy listened sympathetically enough to Daisy's love story, but seemed to be thinking of something else. "I can't go with you tomorrow, Daisy," said Amy. "I need another evening off."

"Your young man?" asked Daisy.

Amy nodded, her face shining.

Daisy hugged her. "Then of course you can have time off, Amy. I'll manage somehow."

But by next morning Daisy was not sure that she would manage. She was relieved and surprised when the Earl again offered his services as an escort. "I'll give you a little time with him, Daisy, but not alone," said the Earl firmly and Daisy had to be content with that.

The Earl and Daisy seemed to be the only two souls in Brinton unaffected by the heat, as they strolled arm in arm into the theater. Everyone else seemed to be wilting. The air was even more suffocating than ever and dark purplish clouds were building up on the twilight horizon and great oily waves were sucking at the pier.

Again the Earl left unnoticed, but at the first

interval Daisy decided to go to the dressing room and powder her nose. She must look her very best and she knew that her face was wet with perspiration from the heat of the theater. She spent a long time in front of the dressing table in the small ladies' room and as she rose to return to the theater, she realized that there had been no warning bell and no sound of returning feet. Thunder was crashing overhead so perhaps the sound had drowned out any sound of the theatergoers returning from the pub at the end of the pier for the second act.

She walked into the auditorium and stood still in dismay. Water was pouring in a steady stream through the ceiling of the theater and apart from an old man who was just putting a large bucket under it, the place was deserted.

"Had to close the show, miss," he told her. "I warned 'em the roof wasn't sound, but they wouldn't listen to me. Ho, no! Not goin' to rain this summer, they says."

"I have an appointment with Mr. Dufresne backstage," said Daisy. "But if I go round to the stage door, I shall be soaked."

"Climb up on the stage then, miss," said the old man obligingly. "Just follow the sound of their voices."

Daisy walked through the small orchestra pit. The noise of the thunder above the theater and the waves pounding beneath was deafening. A gust of wind shook the painted city of Verona so that it rippled and shuddered.

Under the noise of the thunder she was faintly able to make out the sound of voices and walked behind the scenery toward the noise.

Then one clear sentence froze her in her tracks. "Well, Bertram, me boy, You ain't going to get your hands on Miss Chatterton's sparklers tonight."

"Or Miss Chatterton's anything else."

"Don't worry," said a slightly cockneyfied voice, "there's always tomorrow. That's if this bleedin' theater doesn't fall down first."

Daisy looked around the corner of a piece of scenery and into the Green Room. The whole cast were sprawled at their ease. Bottles of beer and meat pies were being passed around. But it was Romeo who drew her horrified stare. As she watched, he removed his black curls and balanced them on top of an empty bottle. His own hair was revealed as thinning and dark brown and without the softening effect of his curls, his high-nosed features appeared as belonging more to the Mile End Road than to Verona. His accent too had changed from mildly French to mildly London East End.

"Gawd," said Romeo. "I had that little bird in the palm of me hand." He took a refreshing swig of beer and wiped his mouth with the back of his hand. "Though I tell you, it took all me Thespian efforts to keep me eyes on her face and not on them diamonds. I tell you, ladies and gentlemen of Verona, ten minutes alone with that little dolly and I'll have them in the palm of me hand."

"And what else will you have in the palm of yer hand?" screeched Juliet.

The cast laughed and cheered and Daisy retreated slowly and very carefully as if from a poisonous snake.

The whole theater shook and creaked like a clipper riding out an Atlantic storm. She could not—would not—stay in the theater for shelter, just to be discovered by these hideous mocking actors. What a fool she'd been. She thought gratefully of the kindly Earl. She would probably find him at the pub since he had been smelling of port the night before.

Taking a deep breath she pushed open the door and fled out into the storm. Huge waves were lashing the pier and great buffets of rain were being thrown down from the heavens. Not knowing from one minute to the other whether she was in the sea or on dry land, Daisy made a headlong dash down the pier to where the reassuring light of the George and Dragon twinkled through the storm. Gasping for breath, her green tulle dress plastered to her body and her hair falling about her ears, she pushed open the heavy glass door of the pub and stood on the threshold.

It was empty except for four of Amy's mashers from the whelk-buying day, who looked up at her entrance. "A mermaid, by Jove," cried one. "Come and sit down, my pretty." He jumped to his feet and came forward, taking Daisy by the arm.

Mustering all her ragged dignity, Daisy looked him straight in his bloodshot eyes. "Do not touch me, sir. I am here to find my escort, the Earl of Nottenstone, not to waste my time with riffraff such as you."

The bloodshot eyes narrowed in drunken dislike. "Want his nibs, do you? Well, we'll tell you where to find his nibs. Up them stairs."

"It's a trap," cried Daisy. An elderly taciturn man shuffled out from behind the bar. "You, sir!" cried Daisy. "Where is the Earl of Nottenstone?"

He gave a laconic jerk of his head in the direction of the stairs. Daisy gave a gasp of relief and ran lightly to the top and stood listening. She had heard that gentlemen sometimes take a private parlor in a pub where they can drink apart from the common crowd. She heard the Earl's voice indistinctly from behind a door on her right and with a great sigh of relief, threw the door open.

The small room seemed to be mostly filled with a great double bed. The Earl of Nottenstone's bare backside was presented to her and looking over his shoulder in alarm were the wide blue eyes of Mrs. Blessop, the vicar's wife.

Now Daisy did not fear the storm. She simply wanted to get away . . . very, very far away. She ran downstairs and through the bar, followed by the mocking catcalls of the mashers and the surprised groan of the old man—"How was I to know. I thought he was a-takin' on the two of 'em . . . "—and out into the rage and noise of the storm.

Uncaring, unseeing, and unhearing, she ran the whole way back to the villa and did not stop until she lay face down on her bed, sobbing with mortification.

Amy, returning late from her night out, paused by the door listening to the muffled sobs, and then pushed it open and went in. Clucking with sympathy like a mother hen, she got Daisy out of her wet clothes. All Daisy would do was cry that she must leave in the morning. She must get away. The girl seemed nearly frantic and a worried Amy ran to fetch Curzon.

Together, Amy and Curzon extracted the whole pitiful story from Daisy. She sobbed that the Duke had given her her father's address and that she wanted to go as soon as possible.

Curzon managed to persuade Daisy to go only as far as Brown's Hotel in Albemarle Street, Mayfair.

"Amy can go with you to France," said the butler, "since the Duke seems to have no objection to you going. But you really need a man to go with you."

"Well," said Amy suddenly. "Me and my husband will go with her. We need to get out of the country for a bit."

Both Curzon and Daisy stared at Amy as if they could not believe their ears.

Amy's large eyes began to dance with mischief. "I'm Mrs. Bertie Burke. The vicar married us by special license yesterday."

Chapter Fourteen

The dusty fiacre pulled by its superannuated horse trudged along beside the Mediterranean. Although it was still early morning the heat inside the small vehicle was already suffocating. Amy and Bertie, who seemed to have boundless energy, chattered and exclaimed over the scenery. But Daisy was silent.

A growing feeling of foreboding assailed her now that her father seemed so close. Her new glittering life had been so full of disappointments and the fact that someone like the Duke of Oxenden would no doubt point out that it was all her own fault, did nothing to make her feel any happier or less apprehensive.

In all the long trek south—the stormy Channel crossing, the brief stay with friends of Bertie's on the Avenue Rachel in Paris, the trains and carriages through increasingly foreign countryside—Daisy had had the Duke constantly in her thoughts. If anything bad happened to her, he would not be around any longer to come to her rescue. By the time they had broken their journey in Toulon, Daisy had realized miserably that she had found her true love and that it was utterly hopeless. The Duke of Oxenden was too big a matrimonial prize to trouble himself with mere Daisy Chatterton, Honorable though she might be.

"Only ten kilometers to go," cried Amy as they passed a signpost. "I was beginning to think the place didn't exist."

Daisy took out the crumpled piece of paper with her father's address on it, more to look at the Duke's handwriting than to remind herself of her destination.

Gossip evidently traveled extensively through the French countryside just as it did in England. "Yes," they had said at the hotel in Toulon, "there is an English milord living at Tappalon. A small village, mademoiselle, about fifteen kilometers from Toulon. He lives in a big house on a rise above the village. Anyone will tell you . . ."

Daisy, with all her school French, had succeeded quite well in Paris, but the broad vowels and patois of the south seemed nearly incomprehensible.

She had imagined the French Riviera to be one long *promenade anglaise,* bedecked with striped umbrellas and bougainvillea—not this stark landscape of the moon where a few stunted pines clung to barren, gray, and pitted crags. But the glimpses of the Mediterranean seen through stands of cypress and pine on the shore side were a constant refreshment to eyes weary of the sun's glare and seemingly endless travel.

"Tappalon," called the elderly driver from the box, and the old horse snorted and wheezed as if it realized it would soon be able to rest its weary hooves in the cool shade outside the Bar Publique.

The fiacre came to a stop in the middle of the village square. Several ragged children appeared from nowhere and formed a silent semicircle around the alighting passengers. They were soon joined by their mothers who also stood silently, their quick black eyes rapidly pricing every piece of clothing on the English mesdames.

"Where is the house of Lord Chatterton?" roared Bertie with true English conviction that every foreigner was stone-deaf.

His audience stared at him solemnly. The driver sat woodenly on his box. A pine-scented breeze blew across the square carrying with it the domestic smells of coffee, wine, garlic, and fresh bread. Bertie suddenly realized that he was very hungry. He stared back at his audience with a baffled expression in his weak eyes and then muttered, "I've got it!" He solemnly produced a handful of gold and generously settled the fare and then stood, tossing a gold sovereign up and down in his palm. It glinted in the sharp sunlight and a reflecting gleam showed in the eyes of his audience. "The house of milord Chatterton," repeated Bertie gently. Immediately there was a babble of incomprehensible French, but Daisy gathered that everyone was now determined to show them the way. Bertie selected a boy of about thirteen as guide and they set off behind him. But the rest of the village had decided to come as well and so they left the square and started up a chalky lane leading directly up the hill at the back.

Daisy's heart began to beat fast. She longed to see her father—she dreaded to see her father. But she desperately wanted to belong to someone. Bertie and Amy were a supremely happy honeymoon couple, but their happiness had only made Daisy feel more isolated.

She unfurled her parasol and picked her way up the path, feeling the sharp stones cutting through the thin soles of her boots, which had been fashioned in Paris only for walking on the thick carpets of a French salon.

They passed a flower farm on the hillside where the farmer was hard at work, dying great bunches of marguerites every color of the rainbow. The dusty ground around his house was stained with great splashes of color like an impressionistic painting. The peppery smell of the marguerites mingled with the dusty chalk and made Daisy sneeze. When she had finished blowing her nose she realized that their guide had come to a halt beside a heavy pair of tall wrought-iron gates. Everyone chattered and exclaimed proudly. The boy accepted his guinea with a jerky half bow and then tumbled headlong off down the road, pursued by the villagers, all anxious to have a look at a real piece of gold.

"Well, this is it, Daisy," said Bertie. "If you don't want to go through with it, we can turn back now. You've always got a home with me and Amy, you know."

Daisy smiled at them mistily, but shook her head. Bertie clanged a rusty bell beside the gate and then the three of them waited in silence. A cloud passed over the sun and the crickets sent out a great wave of buzzing and chirping as if disturbed by the loss of warmth.

"I—I don't think anyone's coming," said Daisy. "Is the gate open, Bertie?" He gave it an exploratory push and with a creak it swung back on its rusty hinges. The drive wound upward, bordered on either side with dusty rhododendrons, pine, spruce, and brambles.

The driveway itself was uncared for and more like a dry riverbed than the entrance to a mansion. They turned around a bend and suddenly—there was Lord Chatterton's house.

It was a large two-storied villa built from brown Provençal stone. There was a long terrace at the front with great arched windows opening onto a large cool room. A scarlet lace parasol lay abandoned on a cane table on the terrace, along with a sixpenny, torn, and tattered copy of Ouida's *Held in Bondage*. Daisy hesitated and looked at her companions. She had not envisaged any female in her father's household.

"Probably got house guests," said Bertie breezily, answering Daisy's unspoken question. "Come along. We can't stand here all day."

They moved slowly into the living room. A long table held the greasy remains of luncheon. Various items of female clothing which should never have been exposed to the public gaze lay in a trail from the terrace, through the room, and to a door at the far corner. The reader of Ouida had obviously undressed in stages as she had left the terrace, ending up by removing a frivolous pair of crepe de chine knickers, which now hung drunkenly from the corner of an over-stuffed armchair.

"Anyone at home?" yelled Bertie.

The silence was absolute. Even the breeze outside had ceased to blow and the dusty pines and shrubbery shimmered beneath the scorching sun like a mirage.

"Why, there's your ma!" cried Amy, making Daisy jump. She was pointing to a portrait over the fireplace. A sweet, serene face, very like Daisy's, smiled at them pleasantly from a heavy gilt frame. "Cheer up, Daisy. You're in the right place, anyway," added Amy as Daisy's eyes began to fill with tears.

Daisy felt the loss of her mother as she had never felt it before. If only that gentle figure in the portrait could come to life and step down from its frame and soothe her loneliness and homelessness away with long, cool, maternal hands.

"What d'ye want?" The voice was a harsh croak and the three spun around from their examination of the portrait.

Standing on the threshold to the room was a small girl wrapped in a man's dressing gown. Her hair was dyed an impossible color of red and surmounted a small, sharp white face. Her pale-green eyes were snapping with a mixture of suspicion and jealousy as they roamed over the elegant, if dusty, dress of the visitors.

"I am Daisy Chatterton," said Daisy, stepping forward. "I have come to see my father."

The girl's eyes flashed from the portrait to Daisy's face. "Pleased ter meet you, I'm sure," she said, stepping forward and extending a grubby hand. "Neddie didn't say nuffink about having a daughter, but then he likes to pretend he's sweet and twenty 'isself."

Daisy found that she was trembling from nerves and disappointment. To judge from the clothes scattered about the room, the girl was obviously not a servant.

"And are you a friend of my father? Miss . . ."

"Miss Wellington-Jones-Smythe," said the girl, without batting an eyelid. "I'm your Dad's companion."

"Where is he?" demanded Bertie after introducing himself and Amy.

"Oh, Neddie's gone off to play the tables as usual. Got a big win, buys 'isself . . . himself . . . a motor and beetles off like a rat up a spout and don't give me nuffink . . . anything . . . for the housekeeping."

"Do you think we could have some tea?" asked Daisy. She was beginning to feel faint.

"Okay," said Miss Wellington-Jones-Smythe cheerfully. "I'll rouse the old bag." She disappeared into the nether regions where she could be heard haranguing someone in execrable French.

"What on earth does 'okay' mean?" asked Amy.

"It's an American expression," explained Bertie, anxious to display his transatlantic knowledge. "It means 'all right.' It comes from Martin Van Buren's birthplace, Old Kinderhook, New York State. The Democrats founded the O.K. Club in 1840 and o.k. became a catchword of the party. Hence okay."

Miss Wellington-Jones-Smythe reappeared, followed by a sleepy village girl who placed a tray on the table and began to clean up the room, stopping every now and then to stare openmouthed at the guests. "Help yourselves," said their hostess, "and I'll go and slip into something tight." She gave a sudden infectious giggle, winked at Bertie, and hurried off. Then she popped her head around the door and said, "It's coffee. She can't make tea," and disappeared again.

Amy carried the tray out onto the terrace and pushed the trembling Daisy into a chair. "Now just look at that pretty view, Daisy, and try to relax. If you ask me, it's a good thing we left our bags at that nice hotel in Toulon and the sooner we get back there the better."

"Now, now, Amy," admonished Bertie. "Daisy's come all this way to see her father and she may as well wait until she does."

The coffee was excellent, accompanied as it was by a large imported Dundee cake. The view was peaceful, showing glimpses of the blue Mediterranean through the pines. Everyone but themselves seemed to have gone to sleep on this hot, somnolent afternoon.

Exuding an aroma of sweat, powder, and cheap cologne, their hostess joined them. She had changed into a tightly fitting gown of green and white striped silk, which plunged in a low décolletage showing the pointed, birdlike bones of her thin chest.

"You can call me Rose," she said, sitting down at the table. "You can all stay if you like. We've got plenty of rooms."

"How did you meet my father?" asked Daisy nervously.

"Oh, that was a lark," said Rose, waving a moth-eaten ostrich-feather fan. "It was on the Channel crossing. I felt so sick, I was puking all over the place. Then your Dad comes up with 'is—his—flask of brandy and that puts me right in no time. Well, he says like he's going to live down here and why don't I come along. 'Course I didn't know then that he'd been kicked out the country for cheating at cards," she chattered on, blissfully unaware of

Daisy's face which had become set and white. "Don't know that it'd have made all that much difference. Quite a way your Dad had with him then."

A cruel shaft of sunlight suddenly shone full on her face, highlighting wrinkles at the corners of her eyes and at the side of her mouth. Amy realized that Rose was probably in her late thirties.

"And when do you expect Lord Chatterton to return?" asked Bertie.

"I dunno," said Rose with blithe unconcern. "If he gets a winning streak, he often stays all night."

There was a sound of voices in the driveway but, as Daisy jumped to her feet, a couple came into view and neither of them could possibly be Lord Chatterton.

Both men wore hard high collars, black suits, and black bowler hats, and seemed impervious to the heat.

"Duns," said Rose bitterly. "Wot's he done now?"

They watched in silence as the two men mounted the terrace, their quick eyes taking in every detail. Ignoring the party on the terrace, they moved past into the living room where they began turning the chairs upside down and studying them intently. They had just started knocking on the walls when Daisy cried to Rose, "Aren't you going to do something?"

Rose shrugged a thin shoulder. "Why should I? Neddie's gone and sold the house again. He's always managed to save it at the last minute, but we ain't got anything left to sell."

"B-but," stammered Daisy. "My father sends me a very generous allowance each month . . ."

"I don't know who's paying you money, but it ain't your dad," said Rose. "I know every penny that man hasn't got. If he'd anything to spare, he'd put it on the tables. Cheer up. Maybe you've got a rich admirer."

"I think you're making all this up," said Daisy, her voice trembling. "How dare you speak of my father in such terms. . . ."

But Rose had turned an indifferent shoulder and her averted face spoke volumes to Bertie and Amy. Rose had heard it all before. She then got to her feet and berated the two men in her cockney French, finally driving them off with a torrent of abuse that no English primer could possibly translate.

"Let's get out of here," Bertie was beginning to plead when they all heard the faint sound of a motorcar in the distance.

"The traveler returns," said Rose. "I'd better get the decanter."

Amy, Bertie, and Daisy sat as if turned to stone, as the sound of the motorcar came nearer. The sky turned a milky gray through which the sun still blazed, diffusing a yellow light over the landscape. The motor rolled to a stop outside the terrace. Lord Chatterton gave a hunted look at the three figures on the terrace and bolted around the side of the house and disappeared.

Then sounds of an angry altercation assailed the ears of the three. For a time the words were mercifully indistinct until Lord Chatterton's voice resounded through the house with painful clarity. "Tell her I've left. Tell her anything. I don't want any daughter sponging off me."

White-faced, Daisy got to her feet as the door opened. Lord Chatterton stood on the threshold. He looked Daisy up and down and then sat in an armchair with his back to the terrace.

He was a thin, dapper man dressed in a checkered suit and spats. He had a surprisingly youthful face and a thick head of soft brown hair, very like Daisy's own.

"I'm leaving, Father," said Daisy, addressing the back of the armchair.

"It ain't that I'm not glad to see you," remarked Lord Chatterton. "But I just haven't got any money to support you and that's a fact."

He suddenly twisted around and surveyed his daughter. "You're as pretty as your mother. Thought Angela and David would have married you off by now."

"I do not wish to marry for money," said Daisy coldly. It all seemed like a nightmare. She couldn't possibly be carrying on this sort of conversation with her own father.

He got to his feet and surveyed her with a

sort of leisurely insolence. "Well, now, that's a pretty penny you've got on your back. I must say the Nottenstones have been surprisingly generous."

Daisy faltered, "B—but you have been sending me a very handsome allowance."

He looked at her and began to laugh, "Not me, my dear. I haven't a penny. Your fairy godmother ain't me."

"But Mr. Curzon—the Nottenstones' butler—told me that you . . ."

"Curzon, eh. Used to work for me. Crafty fellow. Some masher's probably got his eye on you and Curzon's setting you up."

For the first time Daisy passionately wished the grim figure of Sara Jenkins back from the grave. Bullying and stern though she may have been, she had been respectability personified.

In one moment Daisy Chatterton finally grew up. Her childish face seemed to harden and mature as she faced her father in the darkening room. Bertie and Amy, who had expected her to break down, stared at her in surprise.

"Mr. Curzon," began Daisy in a cold icy voice, "has been like a father to me. So much so that I had always dreamed you would be something the same. But now," her eyes raked him up and down, "I find *you*. I did not look for perfection, believe me, but it is rather a shock to find myself confronted by a—an *elderly roué*."

Lord Chatterton gave a short bark of laughter.

"There ain't nothing you can say that ain't been said to me before."

"I am going to leave. Please convey my apologies to Miss Wellington-Jones-Smythe."

"Who the hell's she? Oh, *Rose*. What a name. She's plain Rose Smith of Stepney."

"You couldn't leave poor Rose her little bit of social pretense, could you," Daisy spat at him.

"Arrrch! Just like your mother," sneered his lordship. "Always nagging and preaching and . . ."

That was as far as he got, however, because Bertie Burke punched him in the mouth and then stood looking at his own fist as if he couldn't believe it.

Lord Chatterton stood laughing at them, the blood running in two rivulets down his chin. He looked like a middle-aged and very English Count Dracula.

"Look at your faces," he crowed. "What did you expect me to do, gather my daughter to my bosom? Bah! Get back to the Haymarket Theater where you all belong."

Rose had appeared in time to hear the last sentence. "Nobody's going anywhere, Neddie," she snapped. "There's a storm coming up. Me bunion says so and it's never wrong. I've got you ever such a nice room ready, Daisy. Don't mind 'is nibs. Like a bleedin' child, ain't you, Neddie. Now come along o' me, Daisy."

Daisy and Amy followed her from the room, glad of any escape from Lord Chatterton's presence. Rose led them upstairs and into a large whitewashed room. She flung open the shutters and they could hear the faraway rumble of thunder and the sudden hiss of rain. A cool piney breeze wafted into the room like a blessing.

Rose turned with her back to the window. "Don't take it too hard, Daisy. He feels guilty about you so that's why he wants you to leave." When Daisy did not reply, she left, taking Amy with her to show her her room.

Daisy sat for a long time listening to the storm outside. Somehow she found she was beginning to have a feeling of relief. The dreaded meeting with her father was over. There! She had admitted it. Dreaded.

There had been too many odd looks, too many whispers in London society about him for Daisy not to have realized that her father was not exactly popular. Disappointed in love, she had clung to another love only to find it as empty as all the others. But she had to admit that deep within her, she had been expecting it all along.

The rain had stopped beating down and far away in the distance, the thunder rolled its retreat. She rested her head on the windowsill and gazed out over the moonlit Mediterranean. The dingy, sooty London streets seemed very far away.

She began to wonder if she would ever see the Duke of Oxenden again.

True love, she had found, did exist. Because she loved the Duke. But she knew now that she would never find a love like hers that was returned. In her newfound maturity she realized—sadly and undramatically—that she would probably love the handsome Duke until the day she died.

There was a small, beautiful escritoire over by the far wall. She sat down and began to write a letter to Curzon, demanding to know the name of her benefactor. After she had finished, she sat looking at the letter for a few moments and then quickly, taking a small pair of scissors from her reticule, cut off a lock of her hair. She added a P.S.: *Please give this to the Duke of Oxenden,* and then sealed the letter before she could change her mind.

A few days later, the Duke's high-sprung brougham clattered up the long driveway to Marsden Castle. The Duke's gloved hands held the reins lightly and he looked almost wistfully around the surrounding woods as if expecting a demure schoolgirl with her hair in braids to emerge.

He should never have let her go off to France. Never. God knows what she was experiencing now. Daisy Chatterton had no more guards against the sophisticated cruelties of society than . . . dammit, than a kitten. Every time he thought of her, he experienced a small aching pang of loss. Why, for all he knew, she could be safely in the arms of some handsome Comte!

Curzon opened the door. He took the Duke's hat and gloves and looked as if he were about to speak, but Angela came floating into the hallway and bore the Duke off to the garden.

The Earl was reading the morning paper. He put it down at the Duke's approach and gave him an unwelcoming glare.

"What brings you here, Oxenden?"

The Duke sat down at the other side of the table and helped himself to toast. "I came to find out if you have had any news of Miss Chatterton."

"Not a word," said Angela with a giggle, "but you'll never guess what!"

"What?" asked the Duke coldly.

"Well . . . Anne Samson was visiting Cannes with some friends and she thought she would drop in on Neddie on the road. You'll never believe it, but he is living in the most awful squalor with some cockney child who *smells. And* he hasn't changed a bit. He insisted on making up a four at bridge before they left and he took an awful lot of money from them and Anne swears the deck was *marked.*"

"Why didn't you try to stop Daisy from going?"

"She didn't ask us, did she, Davy?" said Angela simply. "It was after that awful storm in Brinton. The servants say she came in dripping with water and looking like a ghost. Davy says she didn't even wait for him after the theater."

The Duke looked at the Earl and the Earl unmistakably blushed. The Duke felt he should have stopped her himself, but he had been so jealous of her infatuation for that posturing actor. That was it, he realized. He had at last admitted it. He had been jealous!

The Earl was saying something, Angela was exclaiming, but the Duke sat as if turned to stone. He loved the girl. He actually was in love with Daisy Chatterton. His host and hostess were beginning to throw the breakfast things at each other, but the Duke sat on bemused, until a plate of kippers narrowly missed his head. He decided to go in search of Curzon.

The butler drew him into the comparative privacy of the pantry. "I have something for you, Your Grace," said Curzon. He mutely held out a lock of soft brown hair. The Duke's heart gave a painful lurch.

"And that's not all," went on the butler. "Her father did tell her that it was not he who was paying the allowance and suggested that I might be in the pay of some masher to . . . er . . . set Miss Chatterton up."

"How cruel we all are," murmured the Duke. "How thoughtlessly cruel. Poor child."

With a weary grimace he said, "You'd better write and tell her the truth . . . about the money."

Curzon hesitated. "Your Grace, I do not wish to be considered impertinent, but I am very fond of Miss Chatterton, very fond indeed. I always considered myself to be a sort of father to her and now that her own father has proved so useless,

I feel it my duty to ask Your Grace your intentions."

"Entirely honorable—I mean marriage." And seeing the look on Curzon's face, he added, "I have only just realized that myself, Curzon, or I would never have let her go."

Curzon stood with his head bowed, fingering the edge of the table.

"Now what's the matter?" asked the Duke.

"Well, Your Grace, I have heard it rumored that your butler is considering retiring and . . ."

"The job is yours, Curzon, any time you like. In fact old Hennessey would probably like you to start right away. He was butler to my father before me, you know—of course, I forgot, you used to work for him—anyway, he'd be very glad of a helping hand."

"Quite, Your Grace."

"Now what?" asked the Duke as Curzon started to stare at the table again.

"If I was to leave this employ promptly, Your Grace, I would then be free to accompany Your Grace to the South of France."

"So you would," said His Grace, with a sudden boyish grin. Then a shadow crossed his face, "What if she has left?"

"We will just need to try," said Curzon. "And now if you will forgive me, Your Grace, I will attend to my immediate packing and endeavor to give notice.

"Oh, a further moment of your time, Your

Grace. I should not tell Miss Chatterton that it is you who have been paying her allowance. I could . . . er . . . manufacture a late rich aunt on her mother's side who had pledged me to secrecy before she died, and inform her that the allowance is to cease on the day of Miss Chatterton's marriage."

"She'd never fall for all that Gothic nonsense!"

Curzon gave a discreet cough. "If things work out as happily as I anticipate between yourself and Miss Chatterton, then . . . I believe . . . she will listen to anything."

Tendering his resignation proved harder for Curzon than he had anticipated. The battle between the Earl and Countess showed no signs of abating as they screamed from one end of the castle to the other. By the time Angela had thrown the Earl's prize collection of electroplated statuary—his father's mementos of the Great Exhibition—into the lake, the Earl was baying for divorce.

When Curzon finally managed to speak his piece during a silence between the angry pair, they immediately fell to again, blaming each other's bad temper for "causing the whole staff to walk out" as Angela put it.

It was with a great feeling of relief that the butler finally found himself in the Duke's carriage and leaving Marsden Castle forever.

They were to travel to Cowes to board the Duke's yacht, the *Seabird,* and set sail for France.

Curzon began to have second thoughts about the whole expedition. Surely Daisy would not stay long with her father. Even now, she could be traveling back through France.

Chapter Fifteen

Daisy had not left after all. By the morning, her father was in a milder mood and apologized with professional and much-used charm for his behavior. It had been the shock of seeing her, he explained. If she and her friends would care to stay a few days, she could have an opportunity to go through some of her mother's old letters and belongings.

Daisy decided to stay. There was not much to go back for in any case. Bertie and Amy loyally elected to stay as well and Bertie hired more servants for the villa for, as he put it, "I may be an easygoing chap, but I do like my comfort . . . so long as I can afford it, that is." He and Amy were not sure how Mr. Burke senior would take the news of their marriage, but Bertie pointed out that as he had agreed to a marriage with Daisy, he would probably be delighted it was someone like Amy with respectable parents.

Amy had not informed her parents either of her

marriage. Mr. and Mrs. Pomfret held very strong views about "marrying outside one's class."

After a week of trying to lure his guests into a card game and failing, Lord Chatterton left for the local casino in disgust. It was situated a few miles along the coast at the small unfashionable resort of Anribes. But the fashionable casinos at places like Cannes had long since ceased to welcome the English milord.

He arrived back very late in the evening on foot. He had been having such a splendid run of luck, he had drunkenly explained, but then fortune had turned against him and he had to wager his car and had lost that as well. Now he could get it all back if only someone would just lend him a trifling sum. Rose yawned and his guests refused to part with so much as a guinea, so he retired to bed cursing them all fluently.

The next day he was quiet and courteous. He had shown Daisy to a room at the top of the house where a battered trunk held all the memories of Daisy's mother and Daisy spent the day reading old letters and staring at old photographs that drew a picture of a once happy marriage.

Lord Chatterton then exerted himself to amuse Bertie and Amy, taking them on a tour of the little village and buying them a bottle of the local wine and plates of little fresh clams. They were as charmed as Lord Chatterton meant them to be and began to think that Daisy's papa was not such a bad fellow after all.

They went back to the villa where several bottles of champagne were produced, ice cold from the deep cellar. Daisy was routed out of her dreams and pressed to join them.

Then dinner was a lavish many-coursed affair with different wines for each remove. Daisy only drank a little of each. Her father's almost wild gaiety was making her feel nervous and both Bertie and Amy were quite drunk.

Rose had not put in an appearance and every time Daisy asked Lord Chatterton where she was, he changed the subject. They were dining on the terrace, watching a red sun sink into the Mediterranean. Daisy had a sudden overwhelming feeling that the Duke of Oxenden was quite near. She was aware of his presence with such a burst of intense feeling that she half turned in her chair, expecting his tall figure to be standing there. There was nothing but the short expanse of unkempt lawn and the long evening shadows of the pines.

Lord Chatterton was circulating the brandy for the second time and pressing Daisy to have some more, when he suddenly cocked his head. An owl hooted softly from the woods. "An owl," he said with a burst of laughter. "Nothing but a sweet little owl. You must excuse me ladies. I shall take this foul-smelling cigar into the garden and commune with the owl." He dropped nimbly over the terrace and was soon lost to view in the deepening shadows of the trees.

Lost to the conventions, Bertie and Amy sat with their arms around each other and Daisy felt as awkward as any gooseberry usually feels in the same situation. She decided to go and look for Rose. As she moved along the upstairs corridor, she was glad that Rose had a room to herself instead of sharing one with her father, although she obviously shared his bed from time to time.

She knocked on the door of Rose's room and waited. There was no reply. Rose must be asleep. But something in the quality of the silence made her gently open the door. Fumbling for a lucifer, she lit a candle on a small table by the door and held it above her head. The room reeked of patchouli and as she moved forward her foot struck an overturned scent bottle. The bed was empty, the closets open with their silent, empty hangers bearing witness to a hurried flight. She moved quickly back and along the corridor to her father's room. It had the same marks of hurried packing and a strong smell of patchouli indicated that Rose had done it for him.

A sudden thought stabbed at Daisy's heart. Her father wouldn't . . . couldn't . . . She ran to her own room.

Her jewel box lay empty, her small store of rings and necklaces gone. Her trunks, recently brought from Toulon, had been opened and rifled. Several elaborate evening dresses were missing.

Her reticule lay upside down on the floor. She knelt in the corner of the room and pried up a loose floorboard. Her small stock of money was safe. She thought to herself how she had laughed when she had hidden it, thinking she was turning into a typical Sarah Jenkins with an inbred distrust of foreigners.

Daisy went slowly down the stairs. As she had expected, there was no sign of her father. His "owl" in the woods must have been Rose giving him the signal that the theft had been completed. Then she looked at Bertie and Amy with a sudden misgiving.

Both got slowly to their feet as they noticed her tense white face.

"Father and Rose have robbed me," said Daisy baldly. "You had both better check your room. I"—here her voice broke—"I just haven't the heart to . . ."

Suddenly sobered, Bertie pushed Amy gently into her chair and then went out quickly. Both women waited in silence. There was a sound of loud swearing from above and then rapid footsteps.

"He's taken every blessed thing we have, Amy," howled Bertie. "All my money, all your jewelry. Of all the thieving conniving—sorry, Daisy, but after all, don't you know your old man's a downright thief?"

"We will report this to the police," said Daisy in a thin, cold voice.

"Oh, you can't," exclaimed Amy. "Your own father . . ."

"I know where to catch him," said Bertie. "He'll have gone straight to the casino. Dammit, we haven't any money to get there."

"I have some. I hid it under the floorboards," said Daisy.

"Well," retorted Bertie, "it's a wise child that knows its own father." Daisy winced.

"We'll go down to the village," Bertie went on, "and see if we can hire some sort of vehicle."

The only vehicle left was an ancient horse and cart belonging to the Bar Publique. Undeterred by its ramshackle appearance, they paid in advance for its hire from Daisy's money and ambled slowly off along the winding coast road to the casino at Anribes.

Peasants heading homeward from a hard day in the stony fields stopped to look with amazement at the elegant trio in the old cart. Bertie had insisted that they all change into evening dress in case even the small casino had strict rules.

They passed through a village and a peasant girl stopped to look enviously at the beautiful mesdames in their splendid gowns. For a moment her envy was briefly reflected in Daisy's eyes. What must it be like, she mused, to wear nothing but loose cotton in this heat instead of being confined in a hot, fashionable hell of heavy stays and horsehair padding?

Daisy was in no doubt about what she meant to

do. If her father was indeed at the casino, she would have him arrested on the spot. She burned with revenge for the wrong done to her faithful friends.

In all her distress, Daisy could only admire the aplomb with which Bertie consigned their battered chariot into the hands of a liveried flunkey outside the casino. All the courage that Bertie had always longed for had come to him unexpectedly through his unusual marriage. He was always grateful to Daisy for unwittingly having been the means of introducing him to Amy and so he stopped her on the threshold of the casino.

"We'll just get our money and stuff back," he said. "That is, if your father's here. We won't bother calling the police."

But Daisy thought she knew her father better than Bertie and thought that it would be necessary to call in the local gendarmes before they could retrieve a penny of it.

The casino was perched on a cliff outside the small town of Anribes. It was about the size of an average English seaside hotel and the main gambling room faced the sea. Long French windows opened onto a marble terrace. The rooms were furnished in a great deal of dusty red plush with gas candelabra lowered down over the green baize tables, casting the faces of the players into shadow.

The light shone on the chests and hands of the players and Daisy saw at a table near the window, the unmistakable grimy, bony bosom of Rose. She whispered to Bertie and pointed.

She and Amy stood in silence, holding each other's hands, as they watched Bertie move across to the table.

A lazy voice whispered in her ear, "Good evening, Daisy!" She whirled around and gazed up into the smiling eyes of the Duke of Oxenden.

All Daisy's rigid self-control broke. She threw herself against him, crying incoherently, "Oh, my father! Oh, the jewels! Oh, Bertie's money! Oh, my father."

"Now then," said the Duke, holding her tightly. "That sounds more like Shylock than Juliet."

Then everything seemed to happen at once. Heads began to turn, two officials began to walk toward them, there was a loud cry from the window table, and Bertie could be seen struggling with someone in the gloom while Rose screamed and screamed. The Duke put Daisy gently to one side and ran forward, as servants hurriedly raised the candelabra above the tables and exposed the tawdry room to the full glare of the gaslight.

Lord Chatterton was struggling with Bertie. He looked up and saw the Duke of Oxenden and with a great wrench, broke himself free from Bertie's clasp. He rushed out onto the terrace and with a tremendous leap, cleared the balustrade.

To Daisy's horrified eyes, it looked as if her father hung motionless for a second while the casino crowd stood frozen. Then he plunged down into the Mediterranean and was lost from view.

The Duke was the first to move. He tore off his jacket and collar and dived headlong over the terrace. Daisy ran to the edge and looked over. The water far below was in the shadow of the cliffs and it was impossible to see anything in the pitch dark. Bertie was arguing volubly with the owner of the casino who seemed to think it was all Bertie's fault.

The other men and women left the tables and slowly crowded around Daisy and together they all stared in silence down into the black depths.

"Mad," exclaimed a Frenchwoman in disgust, finally turning away. "The English are all mad. No one could survive a dive like that. They are both dead."

"Dead!" whispered the crowd like some lugubrious Greek chorus.

Daisy began to tremble. The Duke's servants had gone to find a boat and after what seemed like an eternity, she could see it bobbing in the water. There was a hoarse cry of "Got him!" and the boat began to move toward the rocky shore.

Daisy ran from the casino and out into the night, pursued by Bertie and Amy. Hampered by her long skirts, crying and sobbing, stumbling and falling, she ran down a small path at the side of the promontory.

The Duke of Oxenden came slowly over the

rocks toward her. He wordlessly held her in his arms and rocked her gently to-and-fro like a child.

"I couldn't find him," he said, after a long time. "I couldn't find him. I searched and searched. There may still be hope. Was your father a strong swimmer?"

"I know very little about him," choked Daisy. "Oh, what will I do?"

The water from his sodden clothes was soaking her dress, but Daisy held him very tightly, the only safe refuge in a world that had gone mad.

He gently disengaged himself. "Curzon is waiting in my yacht, Daisy. My servants will move your belongings on board. You belong to me, now, and I will take care of you for the rest of your life. We will be married as soon as possible. I love you, Daisy, and no one will ever hurt you or frighten you again."

Chapter Sixteen

Curzon gave the sherry glasses a final polish and arrayed them on a silver salver, ready to be carried into the drawing room. Nearly a year had passed since the horrifying episode at Anribes. Curzon reflected with satisfaction on the pleasure of working for a happily married couple. The new Duchess was so much in love with her husband, she seemed to glow from within. And the Duke of Oxenden . . . well, he was pretty much in the same state as his wife. There was merit, thought Curzon, in settling for the real thing. Not like poor Amy Burke. Her husband was still always head over heels in love with some woman or another. But, reflected Curzon, Amy was a realist. Bertie always came back to her, she said.

The Duke's stately home, Weatherby, seemed to glow in the late afternoon sunlight. The old Georgian house had taken on a new life as the Duchess's laughter rang through the rooms and her love and happiness communicated themselves to all who came in touch with her. Even the Earl and Countess of Nottenstone ceased to battle and philander when they came on a visit.

Curzon carried the tray of glasses into the drawing room. The London Season was once again in full swing, but the Duke and Duchess had elected to stay in the country. The former Daisy Chatterton sat by the long, open windows, looking out dreamily over the lawns. Her marriage had changed her from a childish girl into a mature woman. Her husband was sitting at his desk working on his estate books. He raised his head and smiled across at Daisy as Curzon came into the room; that special intimate smile of his that always took away her breath.

Curzon set the tray down on the table and began to pour the sherry. "I see Your Grace has not yet read the *Times,*" he remarked anxiously.

"Am I keeping it from you, Curzon?" teased the Duke. "Take it away. I will catch up with the news tomorrow. Oh, wait a minute. Let's see if any of our friends are getting married, engaged, or buried. Now, where's the social column. Ah, yes . . . *Good God*!"

"What is it?" cried Daisy, starting to her feet.

The Duke continued to stare at the social column as if he couldn't believe his eyes. "Why, it must be a joke—" he started, and then—"Why, the old *rascal*." He raised his head. "Come here, Daisy. I'm afraid this is going to be a shock. No—don't go away, Curzon. I want you to hear this as well. A marriage is announced between Ann Gore-Brookes and—and Lord Chatterton!"

"It's not possible," gasped Daisy.

"We never found the body, you know," said the Duke. "It seems as if your father was a strong swimmer after all."

"Where were they married?"

"In Paris," said the Duke.

"Oh, poor Rose," said Daisy.

"Poor Rose nothing," said her husband reading on. "Maid of honor was Miss Rose Wellington-Jones-Smythe. Ann Gore-Brookes is very rich, you know."

Daisy gave a shudder. "To think that I could have married someone like my father . . . with his mistress holding up my wedding train and not even been aware . . . oh, we must warn Ann."

The Duke shook his head. "Under the girlish tee-hee exterior of Ann Gore-Brookes lies a heart of iron. Once Ann is safely wed to your father, Rose will be paid off and I doubt if your Papa will be able to set foot in another casino again. Now," he teased, his golden eyes alight with mischief, "aren't you glad you've got me?"

"Yes," said Daisy simply, throwing herself into his arms as he rose from the desk.

Curzon coughed discreetly and rattled the tray, but the ducal couple were oblivious to anyone or anything else.

Curzon poured himself a glass of sherry and raised it in salute to his master and mistress. And then putting the glass gently down on the tray, he went out and very quietly closed the door.

He waylaid a footman who was about to enter the drawing room with a basket of logs. "Their Graces do not wish to be disturbed," said Curzon.

"Lumme!" said the footman, putting down his basket. "Not *again*."

Curzon shook his head. Servants were not what they used to be. Nothing in England was what it used to be. And then he smiled at the closed door.

Well, at least there was one thing that never changed. . . .